LITTLE LAZARUS

FICTION

Copyright © 2025 by Michael Bible

Cover Design by Matthew Revert

Cover Image *Bathers with a Turtle* by Henri Matisse, Public Domain

ISBN: 9781960988409

CLASH Books

Troy, NY

clashbooks.com

LITTLE LAZARUS

MICHAEL BIBLE

OVERTURE

ENVISION THE PAST. THE THUNDERCLAP OF everything beginning and all the pain and poetry that follows. Space expands, increasing in speed until there is an excess of time and space. So much time and so much space that all possible things come into existence at once. Every choice, every possible possibility. All chaos and all order, too. Now see timelines fork into multitudes. A ceaseless expanding web of probabilities. Now picture a single universe and our own fragile world among the stars and darkness. The smallest cells become complex organs, eyes and kidneys and hearts. Then the beasts and fowl, floor and fauna, increase. Mountains rise and rivers form. Enormous palm trees brush the sky. No human foot has yet touched Earth. Food is abundant, water is clean, predators hunt prey. Earthquakes, volcanoes, hurricanes, tsunamis. Some creatures live long lives, others die after a single breath.

Now find one animal dying after a century of living, stout and slow. Today she would be called a giant tortoise, but it will be thousands of years before any of her species receives a name. She is different from all others like her, wild and lonely.

The first to climb the big hill. The first to seek cool rivers for bathing. She mates each year of her life and hatches thousands of offspring in the century she is alive.

Through her, the gift of dreams is born. As she dies she leaves behind this trait of dreaming that passes through generations of her progeny. A cascading mix of genetics and luck. Her children and grandchildren and great-grandchildren and great-greats and great-great-greats all down the line live slowly, deliberately, savoring each passing sunset as they sink into their quiet visions. Solitary but never alone because they are able to dream. And from this first mother will come two tortoises, one named Lazarus, the other named Little Lazarus, born two million years after her death.

In those intervening millennia, humans arrive vulnerable into the world and become aware of their own existence. They create civilizations and destroy them. Art is invented. God is invented. Sin is invented along with the technology of forgiveness. And through the awful centuries leading towards our own, this mother tortoise's bloodline kept dreaming under silver moons. Waking, they turned their faces to the sun.

Now narrow the scope even more. See only a small town in America. North Carolina early in the 21st century. The streets of a town called Harmony. Full of people longing for something better. Among the empty factories and mega-churches are two teenagers. A boy named Francois and a girl named

Eleanor. They're driving through the night from a party.

Every other citizen is sleeping at that hour except a man in a seersucker suit. He is a wayfarer, a traveler. A common sight in that part of the country until not that long ago. Some were buskers or magicians or living statues. Some were confidence men or hustlers or thieves. Others were mystics and professional raconteurs. The man in the seersucker suit wasn't any of these. He was more of a stroller. In another time and place he might've been called a flaneur or a penniless boulevardier. Harmony nicknamed him Seersucker. He and his tortoise Lazarus moved from town to town predicting the future.

And now they are walking down Mulberry Road in search of a place to sleep. The road features a large hill with a dip in the middle. Perfect for teenagers in cars to launch themselves into the air, a cheap thrill. Driving full speed, becoming briefly weightless. As Lazarus stops to munch a fallen apple, headlights cross his face.

Not far from the hill on Mulberry Road is Eleanor's house, where Francois is driving her. It's a green and yellow house built in the 19th century for the mother of the town's only industrialist. Eleanor's room is on the second floor. Her pet baby tortoise Little Lazarus sleeps there in a shoebox. Eleanor found the little tortoise on a family trip to New York City a few months prior and named him after the clairvoyant tortoise that had come to town with the man in the seersucker suit. Little Lazarus slept, no bigger than a saucer, in Eleanor's room. Down the hall her sister Abby is still awake, waiting for her older sister to get home. Little Lazarus is restless, too. He reaches his nose into the air. Not tall enough to see over the lid of the shoebox. Two signals pass through his mind. First is the smell of the old Jeep's exhaust as it drives by the house. He recognizes it as Eleanor's car and believes she's about to turn into the driveway but instead the smell drifts by and is replaced by another more primordial scent.

The elder Lazarus, more than a century old, waits at the bottom of the hill and smells something, too. What both tortoises recognize, though don't yet realize, is the curious and inexplicable contours of fate. What their cells comprehend but their minds don't yet understand is that they are distant relatives whose meeting was determined thousands of years before.

Francois is drunk behind the wheel, a skinny kid with a Francophile mother, he's tan from weekend tennis. Eleanor is even more drunk. She wears a yellow bathing suit and dirty sneakers, her hair is the color of ripe peaches, her eyes green as limes.

"I'm not ready to go home yet," she'd said. "I want to jump the hill."

And so Francois turned around and drove full speed down the hill because he loved Eleanor and would do anything to make her happy. It will take her many years but Eleanor will realize that she loved Francois in return, long after it's too late. But for now they're speeding fast over the hill. They catch air and hang weightless for a brief moment.

Here is where past becomes future. Two tortoises, two lovers, and a man in a seersucker suit. All fated to this place and time. The Jeep bounces back to the earth and the headlights reveal Lazarus and Seersucker in the middle of the road. The car is going fast. It's too late to stop now.

FRANCOIS

I WOULD LIKE TO GET MY STORY DOWN, OR AT least my side of things, but I can't stop watching the snow. They call this place The Goodbye Hotel because it is the last address for so many, which will likely be my fate too. Tonight there's a fire going in the lobby fireplace and someone opened a bottle of cheap wine so I've decided to write a kind of last testament while I've still got the time. My body is failing me but as long as the fire lasts, at least until the wine is gone, I'll write. I hope you won't mind if I ramble or get a few things wrong or make some other things up. All I have left is a little bit of truth.

The snow is hypnotic and I'm instantly back there. Twenty-five years ago in Harmony. I'm back there again driving alone to the lake with the top down in my father's old Buick convertible. I blasted past pine trees as big as skyscrapers and pulled into my friend Adam's lake house. His father was a mustachioed champion tennis player and the town had high hopes for Adam. One summer he was ranked. I remember Saturdays at the courts. No one could touch him for months. He had some magic spin he could perform when needed. A genius that manifested on breakpoints. He beat everyone his age in the South and was winning his way through a qualifying tournament when his mother died. Something sudden. Heart attack or stroke. Last I heard he was still living back home with his father, working on a landscaping crew. But I remember him before he was broken. When life still offered triumphs. His serve spun past his opponents clean. Tan and tall. Smiling at some girl in the bleachers. Blowing her a kiss before every serve. I can see him so clearly, blond hair and brown eyes, and we are taking his boat out fishing. We were out there on the water catching little ones and throwing them back. When it was time to leave, Adam started the motor but it sputtered to a stop. He tried it again. Nothing. It was getting dark and fewer and fewer boats were passing the cove. It was hard to see us tucked back behind the cypress. We had no paddles, nothing. After about ten minutes a jet ski passed and we started to scream. We thought it would stop, but it drove on. I remember how quiet it was. The darkness was peaceful and terrifying. Finally, a ski boat entered the cove. It towed us to a nearby dock where an older couple were enjoying a glass of wine. We tied up and the gray-haired man gave us gas and we thanked him. Adam offered to pay but the old man turned him down. They started talking and realized he was a former tennis partner of Adam's father. I sat on the dock listening to them catch up. Dipping my toes in the cold water. The reflection in the lake made two moons. I was tired and hungry and sunburned. It was still twilight and every now and then I could see a huge bass leap out of the water and splash away. Almost mocking me for not catching him. I was watching for another fish to jump when a pontoon boat came by. It inched toward the next dock over. It was a group of kids my age from another school. I recognized a few of them from sports. In the back was a girl in a yellow bathing suit. It was Eleanor. The boat reached the dock and tied up. The kids all walked up to the house. Eleanor stood on the dock and looked my way. She was thin and looked nothing like the girl I'd met years before in a pink mohair sweater. I was close enough to see her wink. That was the last time I saw her. And I don't know why these details come back and not others, but I can still feel the cold water on my toes and the way she walked away and the wind off the lake tossing my hair.

Eleanor went missing in August or maybe early September. She was on her way to move into college. They were supposed to leave that afternoon. Eleanor's car was packed up in the driveway. A red Jeep. Her mom was going to follow her to campus in the van and help her unpack. The night before the whole family, her mom and dad and little sister Abby, all went to the Starlight Diner and had breakfast for dinner. Eggs and bacon and grits and waffles and OJ and coffee. They sat around telling old stories about Eleanor. When she learned to drive stick, a broken tooth at Myrtle Beach, a Kindergarten kiss, her first. Her mom was frantic the next morning, double-checking everything in the car. Eleanor wanted to get an iced tea from the convenience store but her mom said they could get whatever she wanted on the way. They were late and had a little fight in the kitchen until her mom said fine, make it quick. But for some reason Eleanor didn't take her car. She walked instead, which wasn't like her. After ten minutes Eleanor's mom was angry. After twenty minutes she was furious. After an hour, she began to worry. She drove to the convenience store. It was a short drive. Maybe two minutes. Down Mulberry Road past Simon's Pond. There was no one in the parking lot. The store was empty too. She asked the man behind the counter if he'd seen a redheaded girl, 18 years old. He said no one had come in like that all day. She drove around the block a few times but then went back home. Eleanor's car was still there. She called her husband. She called the police. She prayed to a merciful God, but Eleanor never came home.

Eleanor's pet tortoise, Little Lazarus, sat in a shoebox on the kitchen counter. She named him after another tortoise named Lazarus who came to town a few months before. One day a man in a seersucker suit appeared out of nowhere with the tortoise. They walked the same route to town across a busy highway. Rubberneckers snapped photos, the newspaper did a story. The giant tortoise was as round as a car tire and tall as a toddler. Although no one really knew anything about them, they became a part of the town legend. Seersucker installed himself on a bench in the afternoons. Whether he was mute,

or refused to talk, it wasn't clear. The only communication he ever engaged in was to write in chalk on
the sidewalk, "Ask Lazarus a yes or no question" and
beside it drew two boxes, one yes, one no. After a
question was asked aloud, Lazarus would move to
either the yes or no box. Is it going to snow tomorrow? Will the Panthers cover the spread? Will I ever
find true love? His answers were mostly correct.

A few months before Eleanor disappeared she'd
gone to New York City on a vacation with her
family. One afternoon she was walking down 14th
Street in Manhattan and saw they were selling exotic
animals at a shop. She stopped and asked the man
how much for the little tortoise.

"This one has a strong heart," he said. "Five
dollars."

So Eleanor bought the little turtle, the size of a
silver dollar, and named him Little Lazarus after the
big Lazarus who had come to town with Seersucker
months earlier. Little Lazarus was so small he fit into
her pocket and Eleanor snuck him all the way home
on the plane. Only her little sister Abby knew the
real story. They told her parents that Eleanor found
him in Simon's Pond. They took him to the vet and
they told her that Little Lazarus was a tortoise and
that he could live for seventy years, sometimes even
much longer. They got him a shoebox and every
night Eleanor fed him cactus and let him walk
around on her belly.

In the rush of hours and days after Eleanor's
disappearance, Little Lazarus sat alone on the

kitchen table in the shoebox. He was the last thing Eleanor was going to pack in the car. The heat was miserable and she didn't want Little Lazarus to have to sit in the hot car for too long. From his box, he could hear the commotion as more people arrived at the house. First Eleanor's father. Then the police. Then neighbors and friends. Relatives from other parts of the state. Pastors and private investigators and later, in the more desperate months, even psychics and mystics and con men and journalists. Little Lazarus lay there trying to understand who these people were and what they wanted. He knew that something terrible had happened. That the world had changed. He felt Eleanor's absence as strong as any human. Eleanor was the most consistent thing he knew. The safety of her pocket and her calming voice.

All evening the kitchen filled with more people and questions. The focus of the search became the convenience store. Neighbors came over, curious about the cop cars. Men returning home from work joined the search. People came, people went. Theories flew around the room. Gossip. Innuendo. Little Lazarus listened.

"Look at the little guy," one of the neighbors said.

She reached down to pick him up but Little Lazarus went inside his shell. Even though he couldn't understand what these strangers were saying, he didn't like them. There was something angry about their voices. Not like Eleanor's voice.

Sometimes she would sing him to sleep like a child. Lullabies. Hush, little baby. Don't say a word.

Late that first afternoon a larger search began and the two neighbors were replaced with other friends and relatives. Someone changed Little Lazarus's water and left red grapes but he never came out of his shell. He waited and he listened. That evening he heard the door close and the long lingering footsteps of Eleanor's father returning home after searching all day for his daughter. He sat down at the kitchen table with his wife, who was also quiet. Her sister Abby was silent too. The whole family sat together and no one spoke. None of them moved for a long time. Finally, Abby fixed coffee. They drank without words, lost in their fear.

Little Lazarus's memories of Eleanor weren't like human memories. They touched him in a deeper, more primordial place. Among the thoughts of her were the distant afternoons of his earliest years. Although he had no sense of it, he was much closer to his birthplace than he knew. He was born less than fifty miles from Eleanor's house in a breeder's barn in the eastern part of the state. His first day on earth was brutal and strange. Hot lamps burned above him. He never saw the outside of the barn and only knew the reek of his siblings. All hatched the same way. Once he'd climbed to the top of his cage and saw the breeder's daughter at the door. She was maybe ten and had long red hair. Little Lazarus waited for her to return but she never did. He was resigned to life as it was in the barn. He thought it was the whole world and would've continued believing it if not for the truck that came weeks later that loaded up him and his siblings and drove them nine hours north to the city. The next three or four weeks he spent in a crate on 14th Street. Little Lazarus always sought the light. He wanted freedom. Just like when he was back at the barn, he climbed to the top of the cage for a better view. Then one afternoon he saw a girl that reminded him of the breeder's daughter. The same flash of red hair. He scrambled again to the top of the crate and reached out to her.

"I think this one likes me," Eleanor said.

Or at least that's how I imagine it.

WHAT I DO REMEMBER CLEARLY WAS THE FIRST time we met. I was sitting in the backseat of a church bus and Eleanor took off my navy blazer. We were sophomores. She laid it over her lap and guided my hand between her legs. We were packed in a bus, a youth choir in red turtlenecks, except for her. She wore a pink mohair sweater and mini skirt. As my fingers advanced, her back arched. There was a serious blizzard raging out the bus window but I didn't care. She had red hair. Big dimples. Green eyes. I lifted the blazer up and I could see a bruise on her thigh in the shape of a UFO. Things were about to get interesting as the bus pulled up to the nursing home. Eleanor gave me my blazer back and we walked inside. The hallways reeked of urine. A fish tank rotted on the sun porch. Fake ferns and bowls of half-eaten peaches sat on the windowsills. The multipurpose room had a black piano. The choir took their places and nurses wheeled in the residents. The music started. Eleanor and I stayed towards the back, near the door, and mouthed the lyrics.

We snuck away and found a room with a sleeping old lady. The other bed in her room was open. The old lady must've been at one time a dancer because there were black-and-white pictures of a young woman dressed as a swan. Eleanor took me to the empty bed and kissed me, then she started to unzip my pleated khakis. I could hear the old lady snoring beside us. There was a TV silently playing the news. This was back in the weird middle years without a war. Out the window I saw a bluebird with one red feather. Eleanor was about to take off her sweater when the old lady beside us woke up.

"Oh my," she said. "I'm on the ceiling again."

We could hear the youth choir singing down the hall from the multipurpose room. Then the singing stopped. Out the old lady's window we saw our group running through the falling snow to the van. By the time we got outside, it was driving away.

A few months later Eleanor and her sister Abby threw a party when their parents were away. I ended up alone in Eleanor's bedroom. She jumped around, grinning like she knew some secret I was about to discover. She opened the bedside drawer and took out a tiny pill in the shape of a unicorn and gave me half. I sat at the edge of her bed. We could feel the bass thumping from the dance party downstairs. She moved closer, kissed me, then pushed me away, ran to the window and flung it open.

"We need the night," she said.

We crawled out and sat on the roof and let the wind blow over us as the unicorn pill kicked into high gear. The tree branches like dueling swords. Was it summer or winter? I can't remember. The trees were black against a purple sky. We were a hundred miles from the Atlantic but I swore I could smell the ocean. This night has been mixed up with a million other nights. Midnight trips to Indian casinos. Cheap wine hangovers. Late checkouts in roadside motels. It was all the same night. Eleanor and I sat on the roof smoking cigarettes and I felt the pill starting to go wild inside me. The night became my friend. We held each other under the moon. I don't remember going back inside her bedroom. It was like we floated through the window. Eleanor was suddenly nude. She stood quietly for a long time and then started to sing the Star-Spangled Banner. She took my hand and put it over her heart. I took off my clothes. We went under the covers. She kissed my neck and moved my hand lower. Just before my hand went between her legs, she stopped me.

"You can do whatever you want," she said. "As long as you do it slowly."

Two years later I was in Germany about to fly back home to America, sitting in an airport in Hamburg. I'd been there for a few weeks with my roommate from boarding school. He was a German exchange student. A tall, sweet kid with a face full of acne. The only thing I remember him owning was a huge hanging bag full of wool suits and around a hundred hardcore rap CDs, meticulously cataloged by artist and year. His hair was light blond and his eyes were crystal blue. Our school, Wetmore Academy, was an all-male institution in the Blue Ridge mountains. Mainly for black sheep sons of wealthy southern families. Lots of church and seated dinners. The rolling mountains I could see from my dorm room window were as old as time and near the end of the year I knew every peak by its name. Knew the exact week of the year the leaves would start to change, which rivers blended into other rivers, where the hawks like to nest.

When I got to the airport, I went to a payphone and called home. My dad answered. We talked about what time the flight would get in and where to meet him. He said he was excited for me to get home. Then he paused.

"Do you know a girl named Eleanor," he asked.

"Yes," I said.

"She went missing," he said.

SOMETIMES I THINK ABOUT LITTLE LAZARUS. I picture him on the kitchen counter in his shoebox in the days after Eleanor disappeared. The family didn't cook and barely ate, but food came in waves from neighbors. Large silver trays of lasagna and corn-bread and Greek salads. Gallons of lemonade and sweet tea. Pies of every kind and boxes of cookies. It became a problem to store things and Eleanor's mother had to issue a statement asking that food be sent to the firehouse where the search was being coordinated. I landed home from Germany in the midst of this. The news trucks and the search dogs. Everyone was scared that some kind of killer was about to strike again. Prayer services and candlelight vigils. I went to a few of them, wore an orange vest and searched the woods one humid September after-noon. But soon I stopped going, I was afraid of what I might find out in those woods. I stayed in my room and played drums. It was hard to believe that I was actually searching for Eleanor. As if I would find her in the woods sitting alone saying, "What took you so long?"

After she went missing, she had half a dozen girls in pigtails crying on the news claiming to be her best friend. The days and weeks dragged on. Summer stuck around that year well into the fall and the searchers stopped their round-the-clock response. Only a few dedicated volunteers were still out there in the hot piney woods calling her name. I didn't want to imagine she was really dead, but soon everyone loses hope. Perhaps the police, who had seen this kind of thing before, might've lost faith the soonest. After a day or two they knew it was a numbers game, and statistically she was on the wrong side of it. Maybe the neighbors lost hope next. After a week or two. But the family would never admit the fear of what at some point they knew to be true. That they might never see her again and may never know what happened to her.

Soon it was time for me to go back to Wetmore Academy. I was an upperclassman now, which afforded me a private dorm room. It was strange being back at school. I tried to distract myself from thoughts of Eleanor. I went to the library and pulled books from the shelves on any random subject and read them cover to cover. During the first assembly back from summer break there was a new music teacher. The old music teacher Doc Rob had retired and Ms. Hopper was his replacement. She was tiny and mysterious. The headmaster asked her to stand and said she was a recent college graduate from a conservatory in Tennessee. When she smiled, I could see a big gap in her teeth. Over the next few months I met with her in the tiny rehearsal space next to the library each Friday. We listened to

Coltrane and Howling Wolf. Sometimes she would play me songs she was writing or songs she recorded at home. They were broken country tunes. I would add drums or other times we would go into long extended jams. She'd play a few basic chords on the piano and I'd come in with a beat. When she started to sing, she floated off the ground a few inches. Hovering there like an angel.

We started recording songs together each week and before too long we almost had a whole record. I was also in class with her on Wednesday afternoons playing jazz songs for credit. It was a trio. Bass and piano were two twins, Mac and Jake Mills. One Friday Ms. Hopper came into the studio and told me we got accepted to play at this recital in Washington D.C. A month or so later the trio took the train with Ms. Hopper, and we stayed in a big hotel downtown with the other high school jazz trios from around the country. The next afternoon we played a Duke Ellington song for a panel of silent judges in the hotel ballroom. I guess we did pretty good cause we got runner-up or something and Ms. Hopper bought us all burgers and milkshakes at the hotel restaurant. Mac and Jake wanted to go to the Smithsonian. After the twins left, Ms. Hopper asked if she could talk to me.

"I know this is crazy but I got us a gig," she said.

That night after Mac and Jake went to their room, Ms. Hopper and I took a cab to a warehouse in some random neighborhood. She was wearing a t-shirt and ripped jeans and bright blue eyeshadow.

She was only 24, but at school she seemed much older. Away from school she had an edge. Kind, but a little bit dangerous too. A man in a leather jacket came up to us and Ms. Hopper gave him two kisses, one for each cheek. He passed her a joint and she hit it.

"Y'all are on in ten minutes," he said.

She started doing vocal exercises and handed me whiskey. I took a small sip. It went down easy. As soon as we were on stage, all my nervousness was gone. Ms. Hopper started with the first chords on the keyboard. I came in with a backbeat. I could see people getting into it, bobbing their heads. After the show we got mobbed. People were asking us if we were going to tour. In the cab back home we were like two old friends. Bandmates. We laughed through the lobby of the hotel and as we got closer to her room I had a warm feeling. Like I didn't want the night to end. She stopped at her door.

"Another drink," I asked.

"Better not," she said.

The next Monday at school felt unreal. All I wanted was to be back on stage. I skipped math class and went by Ms. Hopper's room but she was giving a piano lesson. I waited and waited. I wanted to tell her something but I wasn't sure what. I walked to the library and got on a computer. I started to type out lyrics to a song. They were corny and so I tried to write a poem. That didn't work either, so I started a letter.

Dear Ms. Hopper,

I can't put into words how important our secret evening in DC was to me. You were an angel on stage. My heart hasn't felt that wild since my friend Eleanor disappeared. I was in love with her a little. I feel that way about you. I want to run away and tour the countryside, maybe the world, with you.

I was about to erase it when someone walked into the library. It was George, the lacrosse coach.

"You're not supposed to be in here," he said.

He came over to where I was sitting and I tried to delete the letter, but he was already reading over my shoulder. They fired Ms. Hopper the next day. The ride home with my father after I got kicked out of school was five or six hours in absolute silence. We drove by the Nantahala River. One of the oldest rivers in the world and I could see the orange and yellow leaves falling into the current and drifting away. When we arrived home my mother was in the kitchen making a casserole. She didn't acknowledge me. Neither of them said anything about Ms. Hopper. I was never in trouble. They didn't yell or fight. They simply stopped talking unless necessary. To me and to each other. That night I ate alone in my room for the first time in my life. I never tried to explain. I never told them that Ms. Hopper and I never touched, how it was all a big misunderstanding because I began to enjoy the hours, the quiet. I liked being invisible.

A FEW MONTHS AFTER ELEANOR DISAPPEARED, A journalist from Atlanta started nosing around town. He was interviewing everyone who knew her and he even called my parents and asked if he could talk to me. He wanted to know if I'd ever dated her and if she spoke of Dr. Holland. The journalist had interviewed a few friends of mine off the record and they said he was getting close to a theory about what might've happened. The journalist came to high school football games. He sat in the bleachers with his notebook and pen wearing a wool sports coat. Dr. Holland was the only psychologist in town. He worked out of a nondescript ranch house in the middle of a new development on a long country road. Half the town was seeing him for various mental ailments and receiving drugs that supposedly cured them, but no one would admit it. I saw Dr. Holland once. He was tall and thin and wore big eyeglasses. After I got kicked out of Wetmore, I was depressed. Dr. Holland sat across from me in his home office. There were paintings of ships in rough seas everywhere. I told him that sometimes it felt like the world was on fire in my mind. Dr. Holland wrote me a prescription for pills I never took. I went back to him a few more times but it was always the same. I thought he was a nice man. That was the sum total of our interaction.

This was back before the internet was big, so I must've read the article in the Atlanta newspaper at the library. The headline was something like *Evidence Overlooked in Cold Case*. The new evidence was in Eleanor's diary, where she admitted to having a relationship with Dr. Holland. Of course the town was wild with gossip the next day. People wanted to know what else the diary said. One rumor was that in the heat of passion Dr. Holland had confessed to Eleanor all of the town's secrets, and it was only a matter of time before everyone knew everything about everyone. But the main question was why the police weren't pursuing him as a suspect. The police refused to comment on the investigation, which only fueled more rumors.

That afternoon I sat in the Starlight Diner and listened to people trade gossip about the diary. Some said Eleanor was secretly a prostitute. Or maybe it was a drug deal gone wrong. The problem was what the problem had always been. Eleanor was never found dead. If there was no body, they said, there was no evidence. If they couldn't prove she actually was murdered, they couldn't connect Dr. Holland to it. People wanted them to bring other charges. Statutory rape. Have his license revoked. Over the course of the day, his reputation was ruined.

I was more interested in the prospect of Eleanor's diary. What it actually said about her thoughts. Her side of things. Perhaps Eleanor did have an affair with Dr. Holland. Abby once told me Eleanor was seeing him for anorexia. Perhaps things happened slowly. That instead of the torrid relationship reported by the paper, it was much more innocent at first. In fact, by all accounts Dr. Holland was good at working with Eleanor. They bonded over running. She had taken it up on his recommendation. Perhaps the first time was an accident. They were both running the trails in McAnderson Park. Perhaps she saw him stretching his legs on a bench and walked up to him and said hello. He seemed nervous. Were they supposed to be talking like this? Was it okay for a doctor and patient to engage in such idle public chit-chat? Would he have seen her in her tight t-shirt and thought she looked pretty? Would she have suddenly realized that seeing Dr. Holland felt different outside the context of the office? Would she have felt exposed in public with him as if breaking some unspoken taboo?

"I'm going to do the back five," she said.

At this moment Dr. Holland was faced with a choice. Does he simply say he was running the other way? That he was going to keep it light today and do two miles around the pond? Or maybe he didn't see his response with as much importance. How big a deal could it be? Perhaps he could have a session with her as they ran. It could be a positive thing, a bit unorthodox, but what harm could it do?

"I'll join you," Dr. Holland said.

They ran without talking at first. Only communicating things about the trail or to point out features of the woods. At the end of the run they were sweaty and exhausted in the parking lot. Dr. Holland let her use the water fountain first. They stretched in silence. Perhaps Dr. Holland saw the sweat dripping down Eleanor's tanned legs and looked away. He was glad no boundary had been crossed. That they'd simply run the same trail. There was nothing wrong with that.

"Good run," he said.

"See you tomorrow," she asked.

"Sure," he said.

On his drive home he hoped she didn't think they were going to make running the trail a regular thing. He worried he'd already crossed a line and promised himself he wouldn't go back to the park again tomorrow and would keep all communication with Eleanor to the office. He thought perhaps he should call his own therapist and confess he was struggling. He worried too much for her. It was only when he turned into his driveway that he realized she meant she would see him at therapy. The next day in his office they laughed about the runners they saw on the trails. There was always the really hairy guy who ran without a shirt. And the couple who rollerbladed the paved trail around the pond every day holding hands. Eleanor said she couldn't tell if they were brother and sister or husband and wife. Dr. Holland didn't turn the conversation back to Eleanor's illness. Instead he let the session go on as if they were old friends who met each week to discuss things. As she talked, he pictured her body running on the trail in front of him. He was thinking about how she ran. Her stride and how she rolled her feet with each step. The way her body seemed to glide on the air as if weightless. He remembered her turning around to look at him over her shoulder and smiling. He was transfixed with her, and if there was any possibility of reversing what he felt now it was gone. The next week they went running together on the trail. And the next week and the next. Their sessions in his office became flirtatious. He would tell her about girls he used to date who reminded him of her. She wrote a poem for him. He bought her a novel by Virginia Woolf, but she never read it. Instead she wrote about him in her diary.

For many years Dr. Holland ran triathlons. He would mention it to Eleanor on their runs. He would say if she really wanted something that tested her endurance she should bike and swim too. Cross-country running was only the beginning. They started to train on bikes and swam in the pond too. He became more of a life coach than a therapist. He allowed himself to believe that he had healed her and brought her to a healthy place and therefore could take her further and make her even stronger. Perhaps Dr. Holland invited her to a triathlon or maybe she asked or maybe they came up with the idea together. Dr. Holland could help with her bike handoff and water stops. Or maybe it was Eleanor's doing. Perhaps it was her idea to tell her parents she was going to a college visitation weekend at UNC with a friend from church and telling Dr. Holland that her dad said it was okay because he was her doctor and basically her trainer. Perhaps it doesn't matter in the end. What matters is that they ended up together at the triathlon race.

It all started when she got a cramp in her thigh. She was coming in for her second water break. She tried to massage it out but her hands were stone. He gave her a banana and water but it was still cramping. Dr. Holland knew what he had to do. He laid her down flat on her back and began massaging her upper thigh with both hands. He knew it looked wrong and maybe was wrong, but he also knew how hard she'd worked and how much it would mean to her to finish the race. Perhaps Eleanor felt safe at that moment. She admired Dr. Holland and the things he could endure, it made her feel like she could conquer the world. He wouldn't give up on her like her parents or her teachers did. They locked eyes in that moment and he massaged her leg intensely with both hands and she moaned in pleasure or pain he couldn't tell and then as suddenly as the cramp appeared, it was gone. She was back on two strong legs again and off she went. Her time wasn't great but she finished the race. That night she ate tofu tacos outside his campervan as he put up a tent. The other racers were singing songs around campfires and laughing. Drinking beer and telling lies about race times and mountain lion encounters. Dr. Holland and Eleanor talked a little more about the race but both were exhausted.

"I'll stay in the tent. You take the van," he said.

"No," she said. "I don't mind the tent."

They went back and forth like this for a few minutes till he gave in and took the van. He went right to sleep but she tossed and turned in the tent. She knew it was wrong to knock on the van door and ask him to switch now. He was already asleep. But she thought maybe it was getting too cold and she might get sick. Or worse, some drunken idiot could wander over and try and get in the tent with her. When she lifted her head up she could see a light on in the van. Dr. Holland had woken in the night, worried that he shouldn't have left Eleanor out in the cold but was too afraid to wake her. She unzipped her tent and walked over to the van and knocked. He slid open the door.

"Everything okay," he asked.

"Too cold," she said.

I must now draw a line in the sand, so to speak. Because whatever did or didn't happen that night remains unclear. If you were to ask Dr. Holland, and the journalist from the Atlanta paper did reach out to him, nothing sexual happened that night. Eleanor's diary said otherwise.

Teenagers pelted Dr. Holland's office with eggs. The church banned him from membership. When he came into the Starlight Diner, everyone turned their heads. Throughout all of it, he denied everything. Eventually he couldn't even go into the supermarket. Finally after months of harassment, Dr. Holland hired a lawyer and sued the journalist.

There wasn't much news about him after that. No more stories came out about him and he never showed his face in Harmony again. I heard about the rest of the story many months later. I ran into my friends Lee and Lesley. They were twins. I was back in town for a long weekend. They were at Bummer's, the only bar left downtown. The subject of Eleanor came up and they asked if I'd heard about Dr. Holland. I said I hadn't.

"Turns out the diary was bullshit," Lee said.

"All of it," Lesley said.

Lee was playing that basketball game where you try to see how many shots you can get in under a minute. He took a crazy bank shot and almost fell over.

"That reporter was making up shit," Lee said.

"Turns out the diary was a class assignment," Lesley said. "The guy in the diary just had Dr. Holland's first name. Teddy."

"How about that," Lee said. "A life ruined by creative fucking writing."

SOMETIMES I THINK ABOUT ABBY, ELEANOR'S sister. Back home for the rest of my senior year, I began hanging out at Lee and Lesley's house more and more. It was a small group of seven or so close friends and the parties were great. Big lavish catered things. Their parents ran some sort of pyramid scheme and eventually went to federal prison but until they did it was a wild ride. They would be gone for long weekends and the house was ours. The pool and the wine cellar and the golf carts and the big TV in the basement and plenty of beds. Lee wasn't out to his parents, but all his friends knew. Lesley was always in love with some guy who didn't love her back. But on the dance floor the twins did border-line inappropriate moves. They had both been dancers as children. They did outlandish flamingos and waltzes and tango and crazy flips and turns and spins. Abby was there one night. She came out to the back porch and asked me for a cigarette.

She looked out over the yard. Her skin was olive, she wore a green bathing suit. She had a dinosaur towel around her waist. Abby took a long drag from her cigarette. I wondered if she thought of her sister as dead now or if some part of her was still hoping. All these questions congregated in the trees. Already we were haunted and helpless. Our lives were lived out in the backyards of absent parents and the shallow end of pools and driving empty highways a little drunk. We were destined to be lost. And yet, I longed for the impossible.

Abby went inside and came back out with a bottle of what looked like expensive bourbon and took a long pull and handed it to me. Everything was unspoken. We didn't need to speak it, or perhaps we simply didn't know how to say what we both knew to be true. Then she turned to me.

"Eleanor loved you," she said. "But I loved you first."

Then she knocked back another shot and I did the same. Before I could say anything, she stood up and took off her towel. Then she took off her bathing suit and jumped in the pool. I took another shot. She came up for air.

"Do a dive," she said. "But take your trunks off first."

I stood up on the diving board and took my bathing suit off. I was pretty drunk and tried to do some Olympic maneuver. I slipped and scraped my ass on the concrete lip of the pool. I was more embarrassed than hurt. Abby got me a towel and walked me into the house. I was limping, maybe playing it up a little. We walked upstairs and found an empty bedroom. She got bandages from the bathroom and fixed me up. We lay down in bed and she began to kiss me. I kissed her back. She began to climb on top of me and I stopped her.

"Did I do something wrong," she asked.

I got dressed and went home.

After we graduated, we spent the summer at the lake. One weekend I was drunk at a party and asked the girls if any of them could cut my hair. They all said Abby would do it. I didn't know she was there. She'd been in Mexico for a month with her father looking for art. She arrived in the same green bathing suit. Later everyone was gone on the boat and me and Abby were left alone at the house. She told me to go out to the porch and take my shirt off. I sat in an old wooden chair and sipped a cold beer in a bottle. She got scissors and rolled us a joint. The sun made diamonds in the water. She started cutting and lit the joint and we passed it back and forth. I want to say that we had some kind of profound conversation, but we didn't say anything. My hair fell down around me onto the wooden floor. When she was done, she brought me a mirror. A good cut. I went to the outdoor shower and by the time I was done everyone was back from the boat and Abby was gone. Then many years later I found a message from her in my inbox. Maybe a decade had passed since that day at the lake and the haircut. The message found its way into my spam folder. Perhaps because she had a different last name, she'd gotten married. It was sent a year before I finally found it.

"I think of you more than you realize," she wrote.

For a long time I thought of writing her back but never did.

ELEANOR NEVER DISAPPEARED. SHE WAS KILLED ON August 17th, 2000. I was a senior in high school. It was late summer, still hot. Eleanor packed up her car to move into college. She was 18, an incoming freshman at the University of North Carolina, a few hours east of Harmony. Meanwhile, my mother and I were in Winston-Salem shopping for new clothes. I was returning to Wetmore Academy in the fall and needed more button-down shirts. It was late, already dark by the time we headed home. As soon as we got onto I-40 there was a long traffic jam. We knew we were going to be late, so we pulled over and decided to get hot wings at a place called Ronnie's and bring them home. My mom ordered the food and she told me to go to the payphone and call my dad and tell him we were going to be late but we were bringing wings for dinner. I remember Ronnie's. The red tablecloths and the gumball machines and the huge plastic cups of sweet tea. I went outside and put a quarter in the payphone and called home.

"There was a bad wreck," my dad said. "It's on the news."

Eleanor's red Jeep Cherokee was driving east on I-40. Her mom was driving right behind her. She would see the crash and watch Eleanor die on the side of the road. I tried to find any reports about the accident from the time but was only able to find an article written months after.

A man was ordered Monday to perform 74 hours of community service and pay a two thousand dollar fine in connection with a crash that killed two people near Harmony. Gerald Buck, 60, pleaded guilty Monday in Forsyth District Court to two counts of misdemeanor death by vehicle and one count of reckless driving.

Judge Chester Donaldson ordered Buck not to drive in North Carolina for two years and gave him a suspended sentence of 90 days. Buck was charged after a crash on Interstate 40. Bruce Tromel, 42, of Winston-Salem, and Eleanor McElwee, 19, of Harmony, were dead at the scene. Bucks was driving a Geo Prizm westbound on I-40 between N.C. 66 and Sedge Garden Road. He failed to slow enough and struck a GMC Yukon driven by Tromel in front of him, according to the Highway Patrol. The drivers of both vehicles lost control and crossed the median. The Yukon struck an eastbound Jeep Cherokee driven by McElwee.

I remember a longer story about the wreck from the time that had photos in our local paper. The picture was of Eleanor's mangled Jeep and the Yukon. Broken glass on the road. Firefighters clearing the scene. In the foreground is a single pink running shoe and when I saw it I instantly knew it was hers.

I haven't been back to Harmony in decades. That town and my house and the lake and the long blue highways and the gas street lamps that I used to watch all night from the side porch when everyone had gone to sleep. It's gone. In my mind, everything is dark and quiet now.

They held Eleanor's funeral at a church about twenty minutes south of where we lived. Later everyone drove to a state park overlooking the lake. I don't remember the casket. I don't remember a graveside. Only picnic tables full of food and drinks. I felt like a stranger. I sat alone with my sunglasses on trying to work up the courage to leave. I started walking back to my car and heard a voice call my name. It was Eleanor's mom.

"She loved you," she said.

Except none of that's true either.

THAT NIGHT ON THE DOCK WITH ADAM WASN'T the last time I saw her. I sat watching the fish jumping and the moon trapped in the lake. Eleanor came into the cove on the boat with her yellow bathing suit and got off and stood on the neighbor's dock, but she didn't walk away. I whistled and she looked over and smiled. I jumped in the water and swam to her. We partied all night. Played beer pong and danced. The host was this guy named Tim, he played football at the rival high school. He had a big gap in his teeth like David Letterman. Eleanor was beside him all night. He wasn't too happy that I was there and kept asking me how old I was. At one point he flicked his cigarette in my beer but ignored it. I walked out onto the porch. It was late, almost morning. It was too far for me to swim back to Adam's lake house. I sat there and counted the stars. I looked through the window at Eleanor. I was drunk, maybe a little in love.

I keep going back to that stillness. The tragedy is not yet there. I can still speak. I sit in this hotel lobby in Manhattan now, writing out this story a million different ways. All that's left are the trees and the morning sun. The dark branches and the light beginning to explore the water. Later, I saw Eleanor and her cousin talking down near the dock. Eleanor was distraught, crying. I saw her cousin walking back to the house alone. I went down to the dock and asked if she was okay.

"I want you to take me home," she said.

We got in her car. I wasn't really in any condition to get behind the wheel, but it didn't matter. I wanted to be next to her. All I had on was a bathing suit and flip flops and a tweed blazer I'd stolen from Tim's house because I left my shirt in Adam's boat. We drove away. She kept dozing off in the front seat. Her bathing suit strap slipped and exposed a white tan line. She leaned her head against me. I put the strap back in place. She woke up and smiled. It was a long drive back to Harmony. The dark towering pines and the two-lane blacktop. We were in her red Jeep. I played something on the radio. Jazz maybe but the static was bad so I turned it off. She rolled all the windows down.

"Pull over," she said.

There was a small dirt road and I parked the car. She got out and peed in the bushes. She was right in front of the headlights and I could see everything. When she was finished, she stumbled back toward the car. She came around to the driver's side and reached in the window and turned the car off. She climbed on the hood, laid on the windshield. I joined her and we sat there in silence for what seemed like forever. Then I leaned over carefully and touched her shoulder.

"I'm in love with Dr. Holland," she said.

It was dark everywhere. A passing car's headlights washed over us and were gone.

"I was seeing him to treat my depression," she said. "Or my anxiety and body image stuff, you know. I have these bad thoughts and anyway I was seeing him to get rid of the bad thoughts. For a while it was completely professional. We talked about my parents' divorce. I was going through a tough time and I needed someone to listen and he was good at it. Just being there. The change came slowly. It's like the kind of thing that happens without you knowing it. I felt like he understood me. Then one day after our session he invited me upstairs. His office was in his house and we went into his bedroom. And he asked me to lay down and close my eyes. He stood there and told me to relax and I could feel him beside me. He guided me through this meditation and I kept thinking that he was going to touch me. I wanted him to touch me. I thought if he touched me, even just the slightest touch, I would've broken into a million pieces."

"Why are you telling me this," I asked.

"I'm trying to get you to see the difference between you and him," she said.

I tried to kiss her and she pulled away.

"What about Abby," she asked.

"I don't want her," I said. "I want you."

She kissed me.

"I'm not ready to go home yet," she said. "I want to jump the hill."

And so that moment brought me to The Goodbye Hotel through a million lonely miles. I brought old Lazarus from town to town. I never once worried about him. He grazed all day on dandelions and clovers. We hitchhiked along forsaken highways and huddled under bridges in the rain. At night I thought about Eleanor and where she might've gone. One day I got a ride outside of Baltimore from a punk band on their way to play a show in New York City. I had some vague notion of Eleanor ending up there. I remembered her telling me how she found Little Lazarus on 14th Street so I went there and got a room in The Goodbye Hotel. They let me keep Lazarus on the roof. Years ago I used to take him downstairs in the elevator for walks in Union Square. I knew of course I wouldn't find Eleanor there, but in the back of my mind I let myself believe that in a world of limitless probabilities there was a chance, however slight, that she might come walking out of a subway station and see Lazarus and come running over and we would be together again. We would forgive ourselves for killing the man in the seersucker suit. Blame it on bad stars. But that day never came and it probably never will. I'm not dead yet but for many years I've lived as a walking shadow. The fire is out. I should go upstairs and see if Lazarus needs anything. Besides the wine is gone, the snow has stopped, the night is clear. Who knows what tomorrow will bring.

LAZARUS

Lazarus dreamed of Francois and Eleanor as he slept in a billionaire's penthouse. On the 95th floor of a Manhattan high-rise, the penthouse was a sprawling complex of glass overlooking Central Park. Lazarus lived in a large courtyard in a climate-controlled habitat. Except for his keepers, Walt and Sandy, the apartment sat vacant and quiet. The billionaire never lived there and he never intended to. The apartment was a money laundering scheme, a fiefdom in the sky. Lazarus was nothing more than a living antique. More exotic than the most exotic fish, more rare than the rarest bird. The billionaire believed Lazarus was the oldest of all animals and therefore hoped he could grant him eternal life.

The penthouse was 20,000 square feet and featured a wrap-around balcony with a 360-degree view of the city, overlooking the park to the north. Seven bedrooms with 22-foot high ceilings. Two fireplaces, an indoor heated pool, spa, gym, and screening room. The billionaire employed a small army of house cleaners and butlers and cooks ready at a moment's notice to attend to his needs, but they sat idle because when he was in New York the billionaire preferred the Carlyle Hotel.

Lazarus' enclosure was in the middle of the apartment in an open-air courtyard with a retractable roof that sensed the temperature and rainfall and adjusted the habitat according to Lazarus's native climate. It was as if there was a large glass box containing a desert island in the middle of the apartment. Lazarus used a small boulder to gain a vista. On clear days he could see down into the park and watched the ant-like humans walking. The city was almost a mirage to him. A distant and absurd dream. The weather was different up there. Within his enclosure he could sense the unreality of the smells that were piped in, fake palm and simulated ocean breeze. When the roof was open he could smell rain and hear the roar of airplanes crisscrossing the night. In the morning he would wake to find the sky below the penthouse covered in a dense fog and the buildings blanked out as if the city had vanished overnight.

The billionaire wanted to find the largest living male left in the world. He hired a renowned herpetologist and more than 20 of the best trackers in the southern hemisphere to find one. He believed a fake shaman that the blood of the tortoise held extreme wisdom and was likely the key to immortality. The team spent months in the desert valley of the remote Sky Island Mountain range looking for a wild tortoise. Many of the natives hired by the expedition went insane and called for the capture and execution of the billionaire. The scientists spent months in the harsh climate with little to no results and their money was running out. Stupidly, the team had spent their own money with assurances that once a tortoise was found they would be paid handsomely. But for all of the sophisticated tracking equipment and the decades of expertise between them, they failed to find even a trace of the elusive animal. Instead they found themselves on the wrong side of a drug war, and because they couldn't reveal the exact nature of their mission they often found themselves under fire. Finally when the rainy season came and the team decamped for the city, the billionaire came himself to see what was taking so long. In the ballroom of a fancy hotel the team members demanded payment but the billionaire refused. There was a fight between the trackers and the billionaire's private security. He narrowly escaped.

The next morning as his jet touched down in New York City, he was broken. He could feel his age and knew that the years of pain were rapidly approaching if he couldn't find an ancient animal. When he got in the car at the airport there was a new driver. His regular driver had come down with appendicitis and asked his son, Max, to drive in his place because they couldn't afford to lose the billionaire as a client. As Max drove into Manhattan, he asked the billionaire where he was coming from and the billionaire explained that he was looking for a rare animal in Mexico but couldn't find one despite months of searching. The driver's son seemed baffled.

"Why'd you go all the way to Mexico," Max asked. "This is New York City. You can buy anything you want here."

He explained that he had a friend named Dino who could find anything. The billionaire said he wanted a giant tortoise. Max made a call. They arranged to meet Dino at The Goodbye Hotel. He approached their car.

"I hear you can find me a tortoise," the billionaire said.

"I got one upstairs," Dino said.

"Is he the oldest in the world," the billionaire asked.

"He was a resident's pet," he said. "He's in great shape."

"But is he the oldest," the billionaire asked.

Dino looked at Max.

"Sure," he said.

The billionaire rolled the window down a few more inches and slid him a piece of paper with a number on it. Dino read it and nodded his head.

"I'll be right back," he said.

Dino came back after a few minutes and said, "We got a deal. You want to see him?" The billionaire covered his face with a scarf and they walked inside and took the elevator up to the roof. In a large greenhouse they found Lazarus sleeping on a tanned sandstone rock. There were heat lamps and large plants and food and water.

Lazarus saw the stranger from the corner of his eye and knew this meant that Francois was not coming back. His walks to the park were over and a new episode was about to begin. The stranger's appearance signaled in him a deep reservation. Throughout his long life Lazarus had encountered all sorts of humans and knew they weren't always kind but weren't always cruel either. Lazarus hid inside his shell. There was something about the billionaire that he was drawn to. Not the man himself but the fate the man augured. Lazarus brought his head out and looked around.

"He's perfect," the billionaire said.

He called to arrange for Lazarus's keepers to pick him up at The Goodbye Hotel and move him to the penthouse. That evening Lazarus was loaded into a large work truck and driven north through Manhattan. The wind shifted and Lazarus could smell garbage, weed smoke, and stale perfume. The truck rattled over potholes as it turned west toward the glass tower where the billionaire's apartment sat on the 95th floor. The driver was a young man named Walt and his passenger was an older woman named Cassandra, everyone called her Sandy. They had been contracted as his caretakers.

Walt was from a small town in the Mississippi Delta. A lean, tall stoner in expensive sneakers. He'd gone to Ole Miss and nearly drank himself to death at football games. Addicted to the famous fall afternoons of SEC sports, he eliminated pints of bourbon before breakfast and enjoyed large lines of cocaine, or gator tails as his frat brothers called them, until dawn the next day. His father was the former president of an investment firm in Clarksdale and was in federal prison for fraud. Walt's mother was a Sunday school teacher who made turquoise jewelry.

In his final year of college Walt defeated the bourbon by painting. He discovered art by accident. He'd followed a girl he had a crush on to the registrar and signed up to be close to her. On the first day the professor showed the class a painting by Matisse. The work moved him in a way he could not describe. As he walked through the campus he was dizzy from the idea of the painting. The sun was shining in a small blue circle on the ground. A reflection from a stained-glass window in the chapel. He walked toward it and when the light filled his face, he heard the voice of God talking to him. The voice told him to paint with the power of Jesus.

When he painted his drunken desire to watch football faded. The autumn madness diminished in him when he worked alone on the hillside in the open air, painting landscapes. On game days his frat brothers, already wasted beyond words, would see him walking on campus with his canvas under his arm and believe it was an apparition. Surely that wasn't their old buddy Wild Walt with paintings under his arm and a handkerchief around his neck.

One day he received an email from the dean informing him that he was failing out of school. He went to the dean's office to plead his case. She was a short and serious woman. He spoke to her about the drunken fever that came over him at the thought of football and the smell of the green grass and hard liquor and the wasted years he spent pursuing them. It was a real disease that he'd suffered from, and it was now finally letting go of him because he could chase beauty in his art. God had ordained it himself. The dean looked down at an open file on her desk.

"I'm glad you found a hobby," she said. "But you're failing every class."

"The Lord spoke to me," he said. "He told me I have to paint."

The dean closed the file.

"That's great news," she said. "But you won't be graduating."

She stood and showed him the door. Instead of accepting it as a defeat, Walt painted even more. After Christmas break he no longer took any classes at all and simply worked in the countryside painting and he was happy. Then one day his mother called. She wanted to know which hotel to stay at for graduation. Things were filling up and she needed to find something fast. Walt had every intention of telling her the truth but she kept interrupting him with questions. So he told her the name of a good hotel and kept painting right up until the day she arrived for graduation weekend. He brought her to the lime green shack he'd been living in behind a defunct laundromat south of town. He'd painted the walls and floors white and made it a kind of gallery for his work. His mother looked over the paintings. Every bit of wall space was covered and even more canvases were stacked on the floor. She could barely walk around. She turned to him, confused.

"What is this," she asked.

"My art," he said.

"You did this for a class," she asked.

"No," he said. "I did it for God."

He told her that he was behind in a few credits so they weren't going to let him graduate, but all he had to do was show the university president his paintings and he would be so impressed they would give him a degree. Walt's mother nodded. Went along with everything and kissed him goodbye and said she was proud of him. She drove back to her hotel room and called her husband in prison and told him that Walt wasn't going to graduate because he was on drugs. Walt's father made a call to an old friend. He arranged for two ex-Army goons to snatch Walt in the middle of the night and take him to rehab. They came to Walt's green shack the next morning and knocked on the door. They explained that he was an addict and that it was in his best interest to do what they said.

"I don't do drugs," Walt said.

"That's what they all say," the goon said.

"We can call the cops," the other said. "Or you can come with us."

He handed Walt a bag and Walt started packing.

"What's with all the paintings," the first one asked, walking around the room.

"They were painted with the light of Jesus," Walt said.

"You can tell," the first goon said and the other goon laughed.

At rehab in upstate New York, he fell into a depression and one of the doctors suggested he work on the farm. It was a rescue farm a few miles down the road for unwanted and abused animals. Horses and pigs and chickens and cows but also dogs and lizards and a cheetah. Walt wasn't interested at first, but the doctor suggested that he at least tour the grounds. They showed him exotic animals. Two peacocks, a zebra, and a tortoise named Harriet.

Walt began to look after Harriet as if she were his own child. Hand feeding her grapes and taking her on long walks around the farm. He liked her style. How slow she was, how deliberate. She would hear his voice and come to the edge of her enclosure at feeding time. He sang her old country songs. Her favorite was Patsy Cline's *Your Cheatin' Heart*. Walt stayed on at the farm after the program was over and they gave him a job. For many months he didn't think about drinking or football or painting either. All he thought about was Harriet and how much he loved and admired her. He learned everything he could about taking care of tortoises and was planning to go back to school and study zoology, but one day his boss asked if he wanted a short-term gig in New York City. It was just during the fall and winter months. Pay was great. Housing was free. Walt didn't want to leave Harriet, but the boss said he could always have his job when he got back.

A week later Walt drove the truck across town with Lazarus in the back towards the billionaire's apartment. Sandy sat shotgun changing the channel on the radio. She wanted the Puerto Rican station but she couldn't find it on the dial. Walt rolled down the windows and let the night air blow through the cab of the truck. They pulled into the underground garage. Security stopped them.

"We've got the tortoise," Walt said.

Walt showed him the papers. The guard waved him through. Walt parked near the service elevator. Sandy got out and unlatched the back. Lazarus was in his shell, trying to avoid the fluorescent garage lights.

"How are you gonna get that thing to come out," the guard asked.

Walt got out of the cab and came around to the back.

"How old is he," the guard asked.

"Nobody knows for sure," Sandy said. "But the best guess is around 140."

"Damn," the guard said. "I bet he's seen some shit."

Sandy liked the way the guard looked. She smiled at him but he didn't smile back. In the elevator up to the penthouse Sandy fed Lazarus a mango.

"How much money do you think this dude's got in the bank," Sandy asked.

"A lot," Walt said.

"How much is a lot?"

"I don't know, a hundred million."

"Hundred million? This apartment probably cost twice that much. I'd say he's at least worth a few billion."

Lazarus looked at the second mango in Walt's hand and sniffed the air.

"How'd you hear about this gig anyway," Walt asked.

"I saw it online," Sandy said.

"How much are they paying you?"

"18 an hour. How 'bout you?"

"Same," Walt lied.

The elevator doors opened. They were shocked by the opulence. Sandy walked over and touched a couch then sat down.

"Don't do that," Walt said. "There's probably cameras in here."

"What, I can't sit down," Sandy said. "Sitting down is against the law now?"

Walt sat beside her.

"I guess not," he said and motioned to Lazarus. "Here boy. Come sit here."

Lazarus walked close and stood between them and he sat down on the soft purple carpet.

"He really is pretty smart," Sandy said.

"One of the smartest I've ever seen," Walt said.

"You worked with tortoises before?"

"Yeah, this old gal named Harriet. Upstate. She saved me."

Sandy smiled at Walt. She hadn't noticed before, maybe it was the light, but he seemed suddenly handsome. He wasn't really her type. Tall and skinny and young. "I could make an exception," she thought. Sandy had lived in the city all her life, she was almost 63. She'd seen the Manhattan skyline from a million different angles, but never like that, 1,200 feet in the sky. Her father was a butcher on the Lower East Side who died when she was seven and her mother drank herself into disability checks. When she was 18, Sandy moved into a rent-controlled apartment on East 4th. She wanted to be a dancer. She auditioned for years but had little luck getting parts beyond small avant-garde productions performed in East Village theaters and church basements. In the 1980's she'd befriended many of the artists and musicians and poets who congested the neighborhoods around her for the cheap rent. They were runaways from middle America, who lived on the streets or in transient hotels. She slept with men and women indiscriminately in those years and in 1988 had a daughter with a man named Buddy, a brilliant street photographer who squandered his talent on heroin. They named their child Rachel and they lived a bohemian life full of late-night rock shows and gallery openings and once Rachel was old enough to walk she came with them everywhere. There were a few solid years of domestic bliss, Buddy selling photos and Sandy teaching dance at the YMCA. Then one summer night Buddy died in a street fight near Tompkins Square Park trying to protect a teenager from New Mexico who was getting mugged.

Sandy withdrew from dancing altogether and got by on kindness. Rachel slowly began to change too from a quiet dough-faced toddler into a hardened street kid with a quick temper and a devastating right cross. When she was 13 they moved into a hotel near Washington Square full of drag queens and playwrights, cellists and drug dealers. Sandy tried to keep Rachel safe, but the streets were too alluring. One night Rachel came home at 3 am in smeared makeup, high on God knows what. Sandy screamed at her. Threw things, empty wine bottles, chairs, a potted plant. Rachel responded by slapping her mother in the face. Sandy told her to get out and not come back. Rachel stayed away for weeks, living in the parks and train stations until she sucker-punched a businessman and stole his umbrella one rainy autumn afternoon. She called Sandy from jail, whimpering like a child. The next day, Sandy begged each of her neighbors door to door until she came up with two hundred dollars to bail Rachel out. Rachel ran into Sandy's arms and wept and said she would never touch drugs again. She wanted to come home and do things right. Sandy said they would stay sober together. They both wanted a fresh start. They ate breakfast each morning and Sandy took Rachel to school. She got bad grades. Played basketball. Wrote for the school newspaper. Sandy got a job at the front desk of a fancy hotel in midtown, it was just enough to get by. One night she saw a new watch on the wrist of a fellow employee, a waitress at the hotel bar and asked where she got it.

"Let a guy from Milwaukee take a picture of my feet," she said.

So Sandy began to take gifts from men she met at the hotel in exchange for foot photos. The men were from the South and the Midwest and overseas. Sometimes older, often married, always strange. She could spot them at the bar sipping whiskey, looking at her open-toed shoes. She learned to linger until they made the first move. She would listen. Wives, children, work. Then suggest they go to a different hotel. One she knew that was more discreet.

Rick was the first man who didn't just want a foot photo, he wanted to know about her. He asked her questions about her life. He told her he never met anyone like her. She told him about her life as a dancer. How she'd once rehearsed with a Russian prima ballerina from the Bolshoi, seeing her up close, how light and effortless she moved through the air. She told Rick it was like watching an angel fly through heaven. He told her about his wife. How she died suddenly but he still wore the ring. His daughter was at NYU and he was dropping her off at school, but she was with her friends and was embarrassed of dear old dad. So he was all alone. She invited him to come to the other hotel but he said he wanted to see where she lived. He wanted to see her leap through the air like an angel flying through heaven. There was something about him. About the way he talked, the way he saw the world. Something tender and honest. What Sandy couldn't bring herself to tell him was that she had a teenage daughter that she was scared of. She couldn't tell him that she thought Rachel was smarter than she was, and at some level she was frightened of that intelligence because she thought someday Rachel would go far away and do great things and forget about her, and then she would be completely alone forever.

That night, Sandy brought Rick home. He was awkward in his midwestern door-to-door salesman suit. He and Sandy entered the apartment giggling at one another. Rachel was in the living room watching Jeopardy.

"I thought you had basketball tonight," Sandy said.

"Got canceled," Rachel said.

She looked at the strange man. He was smiling behind a red mustache. His tie slightly askew, a little drunk.

"This is Rick," Sandy said. "Rick, this is my daughter Rachel."

"What do you do at the hotel," Rachel asked.

"He doesn't work at the hotel," Sandy said. "He's a friend."

Rachel gave him a death stare and started answering the questions aloud from Jeopardy.

"Who is Albert Camus," she said. "What is aluminum?"

Sandy grabbed the remote and turned the TV off.

"I was watching that," Rachel said.

"I've got an early morning," Rick said. "I really should get a good night's rest."

"No stay," Sandy said. "Rachel is going to her room and we're going to have a drink."

"I'm not so sure that's a great idea," Rick said.

Sandy pleaded with him to stay but Rick insisted he had to go and he walked out.

"Raincheck," he said and left.

Sandy locked the door behind him and closed her eyes. She walked back into the living room where Rachel was watching Jeopardy again.

"What is Machu Picchu," she said. "Who is Lee Marvin?"

Rachel saw her mom come into the room and turned to her.

"Were you really going to sleep with that guy," Rachel asked.

Sandy turned the TV off.

"Go to your room," Sandy said.

"Oh my god," Rachel said. "You really liked him."

After Rachel went away to college in Oregon, Sandy sank deeper into herself. She expressed her despair through karaoke. Four to five nights a week she would go to Sing Sing, a prison themed karaoke bar in the East Village. She loved the old standard tunes from the Great American Songbook. Judy Garland and the Vegas crooners. Everyone else did the latest pop songs or the same tired 90's R&B. At first she wore no costume, perhaps her uniform from the hotel job, but soon she began to get a crowd that would show up just to see her. She started to experiment with makeup and bought a glittery vintage dress and heels. One night there was a rowdy table in the back that kept requesting that she do songs. They invited her to have a drink with them. There were five people of various ages. An older woman, a kid in his 20s, a middle aged couple, and a tall guy who looked like Abe Lincoln. He told her she had a great gift. She sat down at their table.

"So you guys work together," Sandy asked.

"No," Abe Lincoln said. "We met at church."

They invited her to come and sing at a service. She told them she didn't know any church songs but they assured her it wasn't that kind of church. The services were held at people's apartments. Informal, with food and wine. They were adherents of an ancient Gnostic Christianity that read the gospels of Judas and Mary Magdalene. At their meetings they told the story of a human Christ. A shared burden, a common suffering. All they wanted was to hear Sandy sing, for her to share her gift. And they would pay her. She arrived at a Soho loft and sang *Somewhere Over the Rainbow* as about thirty people looked on and sipped wine. Afterwards, a woman in a green sweater with a large brooch in the shape of a French bulldog approached her. Her name was Marge.

"What did you think of the service," she asked Sandy.

"I'm not much for religion," Sandy said.

"Me either," Marge said.

Then Marge touched Sandy on the shoulder in a way that didn't seem sexual or friendly but something in between.

"You're a really sweet person," she said.

Marge told Sandy she was a producer for *America's Got Talent* and thought Sandy would be perfect for the show. Sandy was overjoyed. They made arrangements. The next week when Sandy got to the address Marge had given her it wasn't a TV studio but a four-story walk up in Brooklyn. There was no audition. Instead a group of women sat around in a circle while another woman gave a PowerPoint presentation about selling essential oils, a pyramid scheme.

"I thought you said this was an audition for *America's Got Talent*," Sandy said.

"A little white lie," Marge said. "You're going to make so much money doing this."

Over the course of six months Sandy lost all her savings and her apartment was full of worthless essential oils. She couldn't even afford rent. She called Rachel at school and told her everything was okay and that she just needed a little bit of money but Rachel didn't believe her. She could tell something was wrong by the sound of her voice. Sandy finally told her the truth and Rachel dropped out of school and came home and got a job working at a nail place. Sandy started walking dogs. They were scraping by each month. Things were getting tighter. They cut back Rachel's hours, so Sandy started looking for other odd jobs.

Sandy looked at Walt and Lazarus. They were like something out of a dream. She couldn't believe she'd found herself in this penthouse. She walked over to the window and considered the city. It was so high up that she thought she could've seen the curvature of the earth had it been daylight.

"This shit isn't right," she said. "This beautiful place and no one here to enjoy it."

Sandy went into the kitchen. The refrigerator was stocked with drinks.

"You want a drink," she yelled to Walt.

"We can't take stuff," he said.

He walked into the kitchen. Sandy was selecting what she wanted.

"Of course we can take this," she said. "He won't even notice."

She looked in a smaller wine fridge.

"Uh, oh. Jackpot. Champagne," she said.

"We definitely can't take that," Walt said.

"For eighteen bucks an hour he owes us."

She popped the bottle and poured him a glass.

"I'm sober," Walt said.

"Come on," Sandy said. "Look at this label. That's like a three thousand dollar bottle of champagne or something. You can't turn that down."

"No thanks," Walt said.

Sandy took a sip.

"We should get Lazarus into his room," Walt said.

"Fine," Sandy said. "Be boring."

Lazarus walked toward the window and looked down at the lights. It gave him the feeling of floating. He listened to Walt and Sandy talking in the kitchen. He loved the rhythm of their voices. Over the years he'd come to understand how humans processed things through the pitch and volume of their conversations. Happiness, sadness, anger, those were easy enough emotions to recognize. But Lazarus could also sense lies, guilt, or desire. He knew for instance that Sandy and Walt were likely to make love soon. Their voices betrayed a weakness for the other. The tender melodic way in which Walt objected to Sandy or the way Sandy almost teased Walt into doing what she wanted. It had all the hallmarks.

Walt called for Lazarus. He walked into the kitchen.

"Let's go to your room," Walt said.

They started the slow walk but Sandy stood drinking her champagne. Lazarus turned back. Walt called him again but he wouldn't move.

"I think he's waiting on you," Walt said.

She walked over and took Walt by the arm.

"Aw," she said. "He wants us all to be together."

The three of them walked down the long hallway toward the middle of the apartment where Lazarus's room was. As they turned the corner Walt stopped. His face went white.

"Oh my god," he said and fell to his knees.

"Are you okay," Sandy asked.

"Matisse," he said.

Across from Lazarus's room was a six-foot tall painting by Henri Matisse called *Bathers with Turtle*. Walt wept at the sight of it. Sandy got him to his feet. He took the glass from her hand. He downed the champagne and then he downed the bottle. He kept talking faster and faster. Rambling about how the painting was stolen by the Nazis and should be given back to the public.

"We have to do something," Walt said.

Lazarus walked towards the elevator from one end of the hallway as Walt and Sandy turned and made their way back to the kitchen to get more champagne, just missing him. Lazarus stopped at the elevator unsure of what to do next. He looked at the button, it was about eye level. He pushed it with his nose. Meanwhile, Walt poured another glass and walked back to where the painting hung. It was almost seven feet tall. The canvas has three distinct sections descending from the top. Two blue sections, one slightly darker than the other, made the sky and water. Below that was coral green grass where three nude figures looked at a small turtle. The people were androgynous, one sitting, one standing holding something toward their mouth, and one bending down feeding something to the turtle.

"It was stolen," Walt said. "We must liberate it."

He was weeping, drunk and wailing.

"Are you going to help me or not," he said.

Sandy found a couple of chairs and they got on either side of the painting and brought it down. They agreed they couldn't simply walk out with it and decided to cover it in bedsheets to make it less conspicuous. Proud of their work, they celebrated with more champagne. Sandy kissed Walt. He kissed her back. They were halfway through making love when they realized that Lazarus had escaped.

LAZARUS EMERGED FROM THE ELEVATOR AND OUT
into the air. The smell of freedom was sweet and he
took a deep breath and burped. The moon hung
over the skyscrapers and on the streets it seemed
that people were falling in love or about to kill each
other, he couldn't tell which. The city was full of
strange electricity. A religious procession of
teenagers walked the street singing with classical
guitars, fake blood on their faces. A double-decker
bus passed a fistfight and the tourists snapped
pictures. A police car came speeding by, sirens roar-
ing, through a red light only to park in front of a
halal cart and order food. Lazarus tried to cross the
street but he was too slow and cars began to honk, a
few drove dangerously close to him. A hansom cab
came by and the horse leaned down, smelled him,
and galloped away.

He was happy to be free of the penthouse in the
sky. His life had always been spent putting one foot
in front of the other on solid ground. The soft grass
or the hot pavement, whatever it was, gave him a
sense that the world was full of real possibilities and
they were in front of him somewhere all he had to
do was walk. It was early evening, rush hour had just

passed, and the city was almost abruptly quiet. An in-between time when the offices were empty but the bars weren't yet filling up. No one stopped Lazarus as he walked. There was the general indifference of the city but also many assumed he was a pet, there was already a pot-belly pig in the neighborhood that walked twice a day on a leash through the park. Or perhaps folks thought there was a film shoot and went about their day. Perhaps they would've arrived at the truth that Lazarus wasn't a pet or a movie star and was in fact on the loose, but before anyone could think through what they were seeing Lazarus made it into Central Park and found some bushes to hide under. There was a large rock on one side and thick branches on the other. A little place for him to rest. He wasn't tired but resting was his great superpower. His heartbeat sometimes slowed to only twenty-five beats a minute. The seconds of his life were rendered to him much slower than that of say a housefly. Sometimes he envied the short existence of the fly. He would observe them when he rested, watching with pleasure as they landed on his nose. He loved how they rubbed their legs together like they were plotting something. He thought of the mayflies he saw in Canada one summer, born and dead in a day. How much easier life might be if it was only that long. How much sweeter each second. No more worry, no more plans. Lazarus's years were like weeks, his decades were months and so on. Long and slow and seemingly endless, but he also knew somewhere near his heart that he couldn't last forever. What was the difference between a century and a day when it all came to an end?

He thought of Francois and Eleanor and Sandy and Walt and the others. He thought of his first years and how they occupied his thoughts over him in a deeper way than the bottleneck of the most recent months and days. When he was young time seemed to be more important, but as he aged the years flowed together like streams feeding small rivers which fed larger rivers that led to the great expansive ocean of his memory. He was tired of it all and longed sometimes for a brief bright flash of existence. It turned out it was pretty damned hard to die. He walked on.

From the other side of the rock he could hear voices. He leaned over and saw a girl, a teenager about 16 sitting with an extremely dirty man twice her age. His hair was knotted with unintentional dreadlocks and his front tooth was chipped. He wore designer shoes with holes in them and a fake gold cross around his neck. The girl had short hair, what they used to call a pageboy cut but it wasn't styled as much as maintained. She wore a full face of makeup and long fingernails but her jeans were torn and she had a different style shoe on each foot. Her name was Jill. She'd already forgotten the man's name. They were smoking heroin and she nodded off and woke up to his hands down her pants. This wasn't completely unexpected because the man had paid for the drugs and likely felt he had some right to her or was so high he didn't even know what he was doing. She kicked him when she felt what was happening.

"You think you're so smooth," she said.

"I was sitting here minding my own business and you just kicked me," he said.

The man blushed a little. He was from Montana and had traveled all his life after his father's hands were cut off while working for the Union Pacific Railroad. He was supposed to find work and send money home but he never worked, only engaged in petty thievery and sold his own plasma. Then, when he was in a school for wayward teens in Texas the priest came nightly to his room and damaged him repeatedly, the only sexual encounters he would experience for decades. So he drifted and poured whiskey all over his pain till it didn't work anymore so he moved on to hard drugs to stay numb then they stopped working too so he took them just to stay even. His years in the city were like a string of empty moments that happened throughout the day. He woke up. He scored. He slept. The rest was a blur.

"I was looking for my lighter," he said.

"I know what you were looking for," Jill said.

Jill felt in her pockets for her keys, wallet, and phone. They were all there. Her phone was her most prized possession in the world and she might've kicked the man in the face had he attempted to steal it. She'd gotten the phone for free through a government assistance program. She was walking in the

East Village and a man with an official looking lanyard around his neck stopped her and asked if she wanted a phone. She signed a few papers and he handed it to her. She loved the shiny black screen and the way it felt in her hands. She bought a purple kitty cat case for it from the 99 cent store. She made videos of herself dancing in weird places. In front of a huge sign advertising MRIs or in the middle of the cemetery. Her sense of humor was a little dark and she didn't have many followers. The few she did have were mostly men from other countries.

She'd been selling drugs for a guy named Quiet for about a year. He found her living on the streets and gave her a room in his apartment and called her his girlfriend even though they never slept together. In all her time on the streets she'd remained a virgin, though many had tried. She knew how to fight because her father taught her. He was a middleweight champion in Long Island, worked for the fire department as an administrator for twenty-five years and had a good pension. Her mom was a nurse in the pediatric ICU. They were so-called decent Catholics who tried to control her every thought and action. Jill longed so much for the city that one day she took the train to a rave in Hell's Kitchen and never went back. She looked much older than her age and many thought she was Eastern European until she spoke in a thick Long Island accent. Quiet gave her a place to stay and free drugs as long as she sold them, but lately she'd been taking them too much and she was lost in the fog of her life. The only thing giving her any hope were the motivational videos she watched constantly that told her that she alone had the power to change her life.

She turned to the man beside her now with the unintentional dreadlock, his fake gold cross bouncing in his chest hair. His hands were in the air like a caught criminal.

"I won't touch you again," he said. "Scout's honor."

"I'm putting up a boundary," she said. "So fuck off."

Before she went to bed each night Jill whispered to herself that she was a lucky girl. A lucky, lucky girl. Things were just about to change and she was going to manifest them. But each morning she did the same things she always did. Eat Fruit Loops and smoke heroin. The man lit a cigarette.

"I got a right to sit here just as much as you," he said.

"Fuck off," Jill said. "There something you don't understand about that?"

"I'm one of the nice ones," the man said. "A real nice guy. Can't you see that?"

She raised her fist and he got up and walked back into the park and was gone. Finally alone, Jill took a deep breath and exhaled. She closed her eyes. Five breaths in, five breaths out. Things were getting clearer. "I'm a lucky girl," she said to herself. "A lucky, lucky girl. Things are about to change for me." She heard rustling in the leaves and assumed it was a squirrel and went back to her meditation. The sound got closer and closer and she opened her eyes. Lazarus smiled at her.

"Dinosaur," she screamed.

There was an older couple who heard her. They were wearing matching tracksuits. They looked over to see a girl screaming at a bush and then went back to walking. Jill caught her breath. Lazarus turned and walked out of the bush and toward the walking path. Jill followed him.

"Where do you think you're going, little guy," she said. "The zoo's the other way."

She tried to get him to follow her. It took a few minutes but he turned around going north. He walked up the path and Jill followed behind him filming on her phone.

"I found a dinosaur in Central Park," she said, narrating her video. "Getting him back to the zoo."

She posted it as she watched Lazarus inch his way uptown. She got some strange looks but the park was mostly dark now and not many people could see exactly what was going on. It took them almost an hour to get to the zoo and when they finally got to the gate it was locked.

"Well, shit. What do we do now, little buddy?"

Lazarus seemed unimpressed by the zoo and kept walking. She followed him but after he got a few steps up the path she stopped him before he could go any farther.

"I'm going to take you home," she said.

Lazarus seemed to understand this. For the next few hours they walked north as the city awakened into a new phase of night. They could hear the restaurants and bars filling up. They passed the reservoir into the North Woods of the park. It was wild there and dark and Lazarus for the first time in a long time felt a deep longing for nature. He wanted it to surround him like a womb. The crows talked back and forth in the trees and the grass was cool underfoot. Jill was exhausted. It would've taken her a fraction of the time to get home normally but she wouldn't leave Lazarus's side. As they walked she began to realize that this was the exact thing she had been manifesting. This was her lucky day. All she had to do now was realize what fate was telling her. As they exited the park she guided him toward her building. The traffic was light which made crossing the street easier. There were people getting home from work. Her building was an old pre-war building above a basement Indian market. It had no elevator, but she lived with Quiet on the first floor.

The hallway was full of the smells of spices. Curries and cumin and cardamom. She passed an old woman who didn't even take a second glance at the huge tortoise filling the hallway. The building was full of exotic animals. A man on the fourth floor once owned two tiger cubs for about a year until one of them ate a small dog and the cops came and removed them. The building had a strict mind your own business policy. Jill got Lazarus into her apartment. Quiet wouldn't be home for hours. He was likely at the strip club, trying to get them to play his latest mixtape and selling MDMA. Sometimes he was gone all night.

"You want something to eat," Jill asked.

She went to the kitchen and found Lazarus an apple and made herself some mac and cheese. It was a studio apartment. Quiet usually slept on the couch and she slept on a blow-up mattress. There was enough room for Lazarus to rest beside the TV. She got some blankets and made him a soft place. Then she got a cigar box from under the couch and took from it a bag of small brown powder and dumped a little out on the glass coffee table. She cut it into two lines and took a small straw from the cigar box. Lazarus watched her. He thought there was something pleasant and simple about her.

Memories of other nights spent hiding filled his mind. Throughout the years he found himself on the edge of some strange town, seeking shelter wherever he could. This little apartment was heaven in comparison. It was also favorable to the penthouse he'd just escaped. His worst nightmare was to be on the other side of glass from people. He loved the way they laughed with each other at dumb stories, the music of their voices mixing. He watched Jill snort the two brown lines of powder and nod off to sleep. After he finished his apple he ate her mac and cheese from the bowl on the table. Then he fell asleep, too. At 4 in the morning they were both awoken by keys in the door. Quiet turned the lights on and started screaming at the sight of Lazarus.

"Shut up," Jill said. "You gonna wake the whole damn building."

Quiet was from Arizona. His real name was Quatrain but people called him Quiet. It was an ironic moniker. He was one of the loudest people in his hometown. He was born in the suburbs of Tucson, the son of a long-haul trucker and an English teacher. He went to ASU and began making more money selling cocaine than he ever would with his degree in Communications, so he dropped out. He'd saved up twenty-five grand in cash and flew to New York City because he was obsessed with the Wu-Tang Clan. He either misunderstood the geographical references in their songs or was willingly ignorant of them and ended up in Manhattan rather than the Clan's home turf of Staten Island. He was stupid, short, and bald, but he was a born salesman. He branched out and began to sell all kinds of drugs and was taken in by a local dealer who saw that the cocky kid from out west could get into clubs and make big sales. He'd confided in Jill that he wanted above all things to be a rapper. He put out a new song every few weeks but had only a dozen followers. Some nights he would cry to her about how no one really took him seriously as an artist.

They met the first night she came into the city at Club Ruby in Hell's Kitchen. She was tall and thin and owned the room. Only 16, he found her striking and she found him funny. At first she thought the things he was saying were jokes. A loud, ironic man.

It was only later, the next morning after the drugs wore off, that she realized that was his actual personality. She pitied him, but he wasn't a creep. Other men at the club tried to pick her up. They were wealthy and some of them handsome but she preferred Quiet with his loud absurd pronouncements and his strange boyish kind face. For months every night they were in the clubs. She befriended the bouncers and they let her get the best tables and men would buy her bottles and she could text Quiet and he would come over with his bag of whatever they needed and he would give her a small cut. She didn't go to the clubs much anymore. Instead she walked the park and sold to people who let her score with them. But lately she wanted to manifest something bigger for her life. She never expected that it would be Lazarus. Quiet caught his breath at the sight of the huge tortoise in his living room.

"I'm going to be honest," he said. "I thought a monster was here."

Lazarus moved his head. He'd been dreaming of climbing a mountain at night and touching the stars.

"Calm down," Jill said. "What time is it?"

She dug in her pants for her phone.

"I don't know if I can sleep," Quiet said.

Jill got her phone out. She had hundreds of notifications. They were all from the video she posted of Lazarus walking through the park.

"Hey listen," Quiet said. "I need to talk to you. How much did you make today cause I'm a little short. I owe Sam Sam. It's not a lot. Well, kind of a lot. I made a little side bet on the game about who would win the tip in the second half. I was with all these finance bros at the club. You know, like legit millionaires and shit. Anyway some dude says he'll bet 100k on the Lakers losing the tip and no one will take him up on it. It was my whole bag for the night and he's gonna want his money by noon. So we got to scrape together something fast."

Jill was distracted, still trying to figure out what was going on with the video.

"Jill," Quiet said. "I'm talking to you."

"What," she said.

"Money," he said. "How much did you get?"

"I didn't sell anything."

"I was counting on you to bring me money and instead you brought me a reptile?"

Lazarus looked at both of them. They were animated, flailing their arms.

"We got to think of something," Quiet said. "Think, think, think."

Jill was back on her phone. The notifications kept coming. She checked the video. It had 50,000 views.

"Are you gonna help me," Quiet asked. "Or are you gonna scroll your precious phone the whole time?"

"I think I'm going viral," she said.

"I got to cool off," he said. "My heart is a mile a minute."

Quiet sat down on the couch and took out the baggy of brown powder from the cigar box and cut up some lines on the glass coffee table and did a few. Then cut a few more and did those too. He sank back into the couch and nodded off. Jill scrolled through her notifications. They kept coming. It was up to 75,000 views in just a few minutes. Lazarus watched as she positioned her phone on the table between two empty Fruit Loops boxes so it would stand up. She played a song and when the beat came in she danced wildly around him. The song ended and she watched the video. Deleted it and did it again. This went on for half an hour or so until she got the perfect take and uploaded it. She snorted the rest of Quiet's lines and fell asleep beside him.

Lazarus watched them as they slept. He thought of distant things. The beaches of the island where he was born. The hush of the waves on the sand. He thought of finding wild strawberries in pastures and summer melons rolled off a truck and the rain falling cool on his face. All his life he'd moved. He was slow but always in constant motion. Now he felt no urge to go anywhere. He simply wanted to rest. His bones were tired. He suddenly felt his age. For the first time in his whole life he realized he was old. As he drifted to sleep he thought about joining the stars. He'd heard a shaman speaking of the giant turtle that turned the heavens because all creation sat precariously upon his shell.

Jill, Quiet, and Lazarus were woken hours later by a knocking at the door. Jill rubbed her eyes and checked her phone. Her first video of Lazarus walking in Central Park had over a million views.

The second video of her dancing around him was close behind. Quiet rubbed his eyes.

"Shit, shit, shit," Quiet said.

Jill threw a blanket over Lazarus. There was more knocking.

"Open up," the voice said. "I don't have all day."

Quiet took a deep breath and opened the door a crack.

"Hey man," Quiet said. "We're sleeping. Maybe come back in an hour."

The big man pushed his way inside. Sam Sam wore a dark beard and had large tattooed arms. His shoes were pristine white sneakers with neon orange laces that matched the color of his wrap around shades. In high school he'd been a nose tackle and would've gone all the way, but his brother was killed and he killed the man who did it and served twelve years on a life sentence. There he found Jesus and lost him, then found Muhammad, then lost him too, and finally discovered money was the thing he loved the most. In prison, he smuggled in phones, pills, McDonald's, you name it, and he cut the guards in on it and by the time he left he'd made them near millionaires. Sam Sam was a fair person in most regards but he could be lethal. He'd chased Quiet for money before and knew that if he let him slide this time he would do it again and then others would start to slide too and then where would he be?

"You're short aren't you," he said.

"No, I've got your money," Quiet said.

"Great, where is it?"

"I was with the high rollers last night and you know how that goes. You would've loved it. The girls, Sam Sam. They were all perfect 10's. Hell, a few were perfect 20's."

"Stop talking," Sam Sam said. "Tell me where the money is."

"I told you, these were finance guys," Quiet said. "They're gonna wire me the money tonight."

Sam Sam looked at Jill. She was deep into her phone.

"Where's the money," he asked her.

"How should I know," she said.

Sam Sam lifted his shirt to reveal a gun.

"Somebody here needs to start making sense," he said.

"He lost a bet," Jill said. "He lost it all. A hundred thousand."

"Well now," Sam Sam said. "That's good. See, your girl's got sense."

Lazarus began to move under the blanket. He had gone back to sleep when Jill put the blanket over him but was woken again by the commotion. Sam Sam looked at Lazarus.

"What the hell is that," he asked. There was a knock at the door.

"Are you expecting anyone," Sam Sam asked.

Quiet shrugged.

"Go answer the door," Sam Sam said.

Lazarus watched him with a relaxed bemusement. He knew the excitement was serious but he was long past caring about why. Jill walked to the door.

"Who is it," she asked.

"Would you mind opening the door a moment," a woman's voice said.

"You got a warrant," Jill asked.

"I'm not the police," she said. "You have a tortoise that belongs to my boss."

"You've got the wrong apartment," Jill said.

"I've been authorized to offer a large reward for his safe return," the voice said.

Sam Sam took his gun out and held it behind him. He motioned for Jill to open the door. Jill opened it. There was a woman in glasses in a man's suit with no tie. She was flanked by two large Samoan bodyguards.

"May we come in," the woman asked.

Jill waved them inside and closed the door.

"My name is Louisa," the woman said.

"I'm Jill. That's Quiet and Sam Sam."

Louisa smiled.

"I'm going to cut to the chase if that's okay," she said. "I'm a representative of the current owner of this rare and endangered tortoise, who escaped his enclosure last evening. We tracked him here through a social media video."

"What did you say about a reward," Sam Sam asked.

"I have a check right here already made out," she said. "I can sign it over to you."

"How much," Sam Sam asked.

"I'm authorized to give you up to, but no more than fifty thousand."

Sam Sam rubbed his beard.

"Okay," he said. "But I want cash."

Louisa stood a moment unsure of what to say. She looked at each of the bodyguards.

"I can get you cash tomorrow," she said. "That's no problem."

"See, it is a problem," Sam Sam said. "Cause in my line of business tomorrow never comes."

"I'm open to suggestions as to how we might address your concerns."

"What about that watch you got on?"

"Watch?"

Sam Sam got closer and took her wrist.

"This is a Rolex," he said. "That would cover some of it."

"Fine," she said.

She took off the watch and threw it to him. "Are we good?"

"And the shoes."

"Shoes?"

Sam Sam pointed at the bodyguard's leather shoes. The bodyguards looked at her.

"Take off your shoes," she said.

Neither of them moved.

"I said take your shoes off," she repeated.

They took their shoes off and threw them to Sam Sam.

"There. Do we have a deal," Louisa asked.

"Yeah," Sam Sam said. "We got a deal."

Sam Sam gathered the bodyguard's shoes and walked to the door. Louisa took out her phone and made a call.

"Pull the truck around," she said. "We're coming out."

Lazarus walked outside and saw Walt and Sandy in the truck.

"Hey little buddy," Walt said.

As they drove back to the billionaire's penthouse, Lazarus cleared his mind. He thought of Francois and Eleanor and the night of the accident. How the darkness smelled like lemons. He could almost feel the texture of the seersucker suit again. Soft, threadbare, delicate as lace. Lazarus looked out at the lights of the city and he couldn't distinguish them from stars in the sky. He took a deep breath and exhaled. He wasn't sure where he was going but he was sleepy. The day was almost over. All that was left for him to do was close his eyes.

As Lazarus slept, he dreamed. He dreamed of his companions through the years. There had been a half dozen men that wore the seersucker suit in Lazarus's lifetime, a tradition that had lasted nearly 140 years. They all followed a strict order that was passed down from the first one who found Lazarus in a small Seeker meeting hall in Wilmington, North Carolina, in 1881 when he was only six months old. Each Seersucker wore the same suit and followed three simple rules: They never spoke to anyone while dressed in the suit. Never stayed too long in one town. And above all never interfered with Lazarus's work. Lazarus for his part knew how to bring variety to his answers, how not to show off his skills too much. Just enough to impress but not enough to invite more questions. Each Seersucker would pass down the suit to a new man when it had served him long enough or he had saved enough to retire. The act made more than enough money. Men could make a nice little nest egg for themselves and pass along the suit and instructions on how to care for Lazarus. The arrangement allowed the men to observe people as they were and not who they pretended to be. He could see the ones who were truly in need and when he found the right man, he would pass the suit down to him.

The first was a man named James, a school-teacher in the Tennessee mountains. A Seeker, a pacifist, and a widower. In the summer of 1881 James traveled to Wilmington, a two-day train journey, to attend a secret lecture by a student of Darwin's about the theory of evolution. Live specimens from recent expeditions to the islands would be on display. James had been in contact with the local elder, Kirk, of the church in Wilmington who arranged the lecture. Ever since it was discovered that the Seeker church had harbored runaway families on the Underground Railroad twenty years prior, they'd come under intense scrutiny from local authorities and hosting any so-called blasphemous science gathering would've brought unneeded attention, so the lecture was in the basement of the meeting hall. Kirk wrote to James and invited him. They'd been in a chain letter group with others from across the South who quietly spread radical utopian political ideas, avant-garde literature, and new scientific breakthroughs through the mail. The secret group called themselves Zouave after the French Algerian soldiers who wore fez hats. After their Seeker pamphlets against the war came under fire from the locals, they began to help in a quieter way. They went underground, founding mutual aid societies all over the South for working people. Offering legal help and small interest-free loans to rural farmers, setting up schools in remote parts of the mountains and low country, and supporting victims of natural disasters. The Seersucker operation was but one of many schemes the Zouave started to help itinerant travelers make a living.

The night of Darwin's student's lecture in the basement of the church, Kirk welcomed James. The lecturer showed hand-drawn sketches of rainbow-colored birds and rare trees the size of houses. But the star of the show was a baby tortoise brought directly from their journey. It was a stowaway on their boat, Darwin's student said.

Lazarus remembered that Englishmen had bribed him with food. He spent six months on the ship in a small cigar box. When it was over he was happy to be on dry land. Now he stood on the stool in the middle of the basement as the underground utopians prodded and poked him. The men were full of questions and as the night wore on, the whiskey flowing freely, arguments began about Mr. Darwin's theory and the role of emotions in politics and the fate of the free society. Lazarus took a liking to James. He was quiet and unconcerned with the men's discussions. He was softer than the rest of them, a man of patience and care. Lazarus reached out his mouth and gave James a love bite on his finger.

"Nice to meet you," James said.

Lazarus bit him again. Then he seemed to become frightened as if he could sense something that the men in the basement could not yet perceive. He walked over to James's hand as if he wanted to be picked up and protected.

"What is it," James asked.

The men could hear a strange sound coming from down the road. They all stopped their arguments. It was the roar of a crowd getting closer. They sent a scout to go upstairs and see who was coming. The man reported that a large mob of townsfolk had formed, evidently tipped off to radical science being discussed. The men flew into a panic. Some tried to hide, others made a run for it. James grabbed Lazarus and put him in his coat pocket. He walked upstairs to the front door of the meeting hall and waited for the mob to get closer. When the mob burst through the doors he blended in with them, screaming and running for the basement. When they'd all run by he did an about-face and fled into the night.

James avoided the town square. He kept to the backroads and spoke to no one. He didn't know where to go so he tried to find his way back to Kirk's house, the only person he knew in town. He waited on the back porch until Kirk arrived home. His face was covered in ash.

"Thank god you're okay," Kirk said. "I thought you'd been killed."

"Are you alright," James asked.

"The church is on fire. I made it out, but many didn't," he said.

They went to Kirk's study to make a plan. Kirk laid out a map of the countryside.

"The mob will likely take this road back to town," Kirk said. "We don't have much time."

Kirk gave James an old seersucker suit he used to wear in college and a horse and told him to ride to the next town and he would see him there in the morning. James put Lazarus in the front pocket of the seersucker suit. As soon as James left the barn, he could hear the mob moving toward Kirk's house. He looked back to see the house engulfed in fire.

Lazarus had listened to the mob with increasing alarm but knew that James would protect him. That night they slept in a marsh on the outskirts of Wilmington and made it to a small town late the next day. James got them a room in a boarding house. Lazarus was tired and confused but he trusted James. He knew there was something kind about him as he played solitaire on the bed while Lazarus munched a green apple beside him. For three or four days they spent the night there until James ran out of money. The manager of the boarding house, an Irish grandmother everyone called Lady Hammer, would come to the room every evening seeking payment without much luck until she threatened to put them on the street. So the next day James took Lazarus to a nearby park. People were out enjoying the day. James sat on a bench and took Lazarus out of his pocket and let him crawl on the ground. One child came up and asked if she could pet him. James said yes. Then another child and another child until there were about a dozen or so children asking his name and what he liked to eat. James finally had to tell them they needed to go. As he sat at a bar with Lazarus drinking away the last of their money, James had an idea. He took the chalk from the blackboard that announced the soup of the day and walked back out into the park. He wrote on the newly installed pavement. "Lazarus the Clairvoyant answers yes or no questions for a penny."

The kids told their friends and they told their friends until children from nearby counties were traveling to see the clairvoyant turtle. The first week James and Lazarus made enough to stay the rest of the month at the boarding house, meals included. Each night Lazarus ate his favorite pears and enjoyed a sip of French wine with James. Then one night they were relaxing in their room and there was a knock at the door. It was Lady Hammer with a large hairy man, his boots covered in cow shit.

"Did you tell my daughter your turtle can see the future," the man said.

He was fuming, his eyes coming out of his head.

"Lazarus only answers yes or no questions," James said.

"This is some kind of witchcraft," the man said. "My daughter spent two dollars on this witchcraft. You owe me two dollars."

"Witchcraft is not allowed in my boarding house," Lady Hammer said.

James offered to give him two dollars but the man was too angry to listen. He left but said he would return with his brothers. James and Lazarus fled on foot and camped in the woods. James learned that it was best to keep a low profile, so he stopped talking to people. In the next town the same thing happened. Children came to ask Lazarus questions but this time he said nothing. Only wrote in chalk and put a hat down for pennies. Sure enough an angry father would always show up claiming they were charlatans. But James would simply write with chalk, "deaf-mute" and the men would back off. They would realize this was the only way he could make a living, not a scam but more of a charity magic act. Some even offered him money on the spot. He also realized it was smart to move on after a month or so to avoid questions.

As they lived together through the years and decades, James and Lazarus became family. Each needing the other. They chose to be nomadic, learning the best routes and how to travel on foot. When Lazarus got too big to carry in his pocket, James bought an old salesman's wagon, a kind of enclosed rickshaw, but Lazarus hated it. He always jumped out, preferring the air. The wagon housed their belongings and food instead. It was also just big enough for them to sleep in on rainy nights. James pulled it as he walked behind Lazarus from town to town. Soon, James learned that Lazarus wasn't as helpless as he seemed. In fact, he had a deep animal sense of the environment. James began to move at Lazarus's pace instead of forcing him to live on human time, in a human way, and James began to let

Lazarus take the lead. He could find sources of water easier than James could, he could locate wild blueberries and find apple trees and honeysuckle blossoms.

A few months after the raid at the Seeker meeting hall a man approached them in a park. Lazarus recognized him before James did. It was Kirk, he'd survived the mob. James and Kirk embraced and walked to a small church nearby. Lazarus followed. The sanctuary was dark and cold. Kirk lit a pipe. That afternoon they decided to formalize the Seersucker role.

"From now on you will give up your past," Kirk said. "You will only be known by your suit."

"But someday I want to go back to my life," James said.

"And you will," Kirk said. "All I ask is that you pass the suit and the tortoise down to another man in need."

James nodded and Kirk smiled. Years later, Kirk would become a lawyer in a small Virginia town defending indigent people. On weekends he sang in the community choir and baked prize-winning pies. He was a gentle, quiet man, who worked with his hands but was in touch with his softer side. Above all things he hated war and God. He despised all ideologies. Kirk and James shook hands. Kirk said he would contact the Order of the Zouave and tell them of Project Seersucker. He told James that if he ever got into trouble simply come to a meeting and find a member with the black cross. They wrote often, but they never saw each other again.

For the next five years Lazarus and James traveled all over the South. Telling fortunes, getting run out of town. They only made enough to live. When they made more than they needed, they would stuff church donation boxes. Those first years of traveling were a beautiful dream to Lazarus. Low fog over the mountains as they hiked to a cave to sleep listening to the crickets all night. Or early purple sunrises and afternoon rainstorms. They walked highways and backroads. Kept away from big cities and stuck to the towns and the countryside. Lazarus learned the land. By smell he could remember each place, safety and danger lived in his nose. He had to do this because he knew even then that their time together was short. James often spoke of a coming day when they could no longer work together. That they would have to find a new person to become Seersucker. But Lazarus didn't realize it would happen so fast.

It was just before dark, they were walking near the train tracks on some forgotten piece of land in Alabama that likely had no name on any map, just miles and miles of wild pastures. A freighter passed and they moved to the side. From the caboose jumped a boy of about 19. His hair was sandy blond and his eyes were pale blue through his dirty face.

"Hey," the kid said. "Where are y'all going?"

James and Lazarus kept walking.

"Can I join you," he asked.

James stopped. He pointed at his mouth and shook his head.

"You don't talk," the kid asked.

James nodded and kept walking.

"People call me Simon," the kid said.

James and Lazarus kept walking.

"I sure could use some help," he said.

James stopped. He walked over to Simon and gave him a ten-dollar bill. Simon handed it back to him.

"No sir," he said. "Not that kind of help. I saw you in town yesterday. I want some answers. From the turtle."

James looked at Lazarus.

"It's about my dad," Simon said. "He was sick when I left and I just want to know if he made it."

Lazarus could see Simon's eyes watering a little in the light. The grass was tall beside the tracks. Yellowed from the sun. James took out a small pad and pencil.

"Are you hungry," he wrote.

James set up camp and made vegetable stew and Simon talked about his life. He said he'd been drafted into the Army but refused to go. He'd run away and become an outlaw in the process. He couldn't go back for fear of being arrested so he stayed on the road. Doing odd jobs when he could. Painting houses or shoeing horses. He loved animals more than anything in the world and believed they had souls and refused to eat meat.

"One day I'd like to learn guitar and maybe fall in love with a pretty girl," he said.

Then he got quiet and looked deep into the fire.

"But I want my fortune, I want to ask the turtle if my dad's okay," he said. "If he ain't okay that's alright I just want to know."

James took out his notebook and wrote, "Lazarus can't answer those types of questions."

"Lazarus," Simon said. "I like that name."

He touched his shell. Lazarus could feel something in his warm hand. He could sense that the kid had some time left to live, but if they parted ways he might not see those years. Already Simon's voice had a raspy thinness to it, a combination of cigarettes and whiskey. Lazarus knew this would be the hardest moment of change. Simon would have a lot to learn but he would be a good Seersucker, but the thought of leaving James was terrible. He looked at James across the campfire. His eyes were closed. He was realizing the same thing that Lazarus had just realized. It was time to go. Time to move on. But also to put into motion something that would serve both the Seersucker and Lazarus. Not just a way to earn a living, but a life in and of itself. A purpose. A small purpose for their lives.

James went back to the wagon and changed into a t-shirt and old jeans and folded the seersucker suit neatly. For the first time since they met, James spoke out loud.

"For a long time I've lived on the run," he said.

"It was because of my membership in a secret benevolent society."

"What's benevolent mean," Simon asked.

"Our group was descended from a group of English heretics from the 1500s called Seekers. They were burned at the stake for simply believing God isn't divine. We created God, they said, not the other way. They hated priests and denounced all hierarchy within society. Divinity is the beauty of art and the acts of the natural world."

Simon nodded and looked at Lazarus.

"I founded a small Seeker sect called Seersuckers," James said.

He handed Simon the suit.

"I'm giving you everything I have," James said. "It's all yours. It is a way of life if you want it. The only rule is that you must never speak while wearing the suit and never stay in one place for too long. I will give you money now of course but you will soon earn more than you can ever imagine. Lazarus will find food if you follow him. Let him guide you in everything you do. Once you are done with this life, pass it on."

"You're giving me Lazarus," Simon asked.

"You are now his keeper," James said.

Lazarus looked at Simon, and Simon nodded his head. James walked away into the growing evening and kept walking. He hitched a ride from a passing train in his t-shirt and old shoes. He'd been a millionaire many times over the past five years, but he'd given it all away. He rode six hours back to the

Smoky Mountains. He thought about how people wanted to believe something magical was possible so he gave them a God. His name was Lazarus and he could perform miracles. Of course the truth was he was a simple, normal tortoise. A creature no more or less miraculous than any other. If they wanted to be healed, they were. If they wanted money, it would find its way to them. Only because they were open to finding it.

Simon spent many years on the road with Lazarus, crisscrossing the south. But as the turn of the century came, word of their arrivals and departures began to spread faster through newspaper accounts and word of mouth. Each town would be mobbed with people as they entered. They threw flowers and wishes written on scraps of paper. Everyone wanted to touch Lazarus for luck. Often local politicians would try to woo them away from their work trying to drum up votes. So Simon began to travel farther. Up into the northeast of the country and into Canada. Across wide sections of the interior to small mining camps and railroad towns. Then through the burgeoning Midwest and out to California. Down into Mexico and Guatemala, then Chile and Brazil. Lazarus on foot. Simon with the wagon. They reached the lowest deserts and the highest mountains. They gave money earned in larger cities to starving villages. Simon saw the world. Traveling on huge boats and long trains. Through hurricanes and revolutions. Taking people's money and giving it away.

Then Simon began to go back to his original question. Was his father alive? What had happened to his family and everything he ever loved? Surely enough time had passed and he could return. Lazarus knew the next shift was coming. They started to walk back to America. It took months. Simon had plenty of money to retire. The year was 1915. They were in the Mississippi Delta and set up camp in a swamp for the night. Their fire was almost out when someone approached them. A short man with a long beard and a broken handcuff on one wrist.

"You got any food," the man asked.

Simon spoke to the man. When he did this, Lazarus knew that Simon had made up his mind to leave.

"I have food," Simon said.

"What about whiskey," the man asked.

"Yes. I have everything but first tell me your name."

"Andrew."

They sat and drank, and Andrew told Simon that he had escaped from the infamous Parchman prison but he was an innocent man. Simon explained that all men were innocent. That crime was a symptom of poverty and neglect.

"I only believe in mercy," Simon said.

He told Andrew about the Seekers. About Seersucker and said it was all his if he wanted it.

"But I'm a sinner," Andrew said.

"We have traveled everywhere and seen all kinds

of people," Simon said. "We are all blind to ourselves, doing what we can to survive this cruel world."

Andrew seemed to understand this and took the seersucker suit. Simon brought him to a river and he washed and changed into it. Cut his beard and stopped speaking.

For the rest of the 20th century this is how it went. When Andrew was done with his life, he passed the suit down to John and John to Peter and so on and so on. Lazarus traveled the world. Europe and Asia. The Seersuckers were men and women from every race and background. The wagon, the original that James bought in the 1890s had been refurbished and the suit itself had been tailored and repaired, but everything else stayed the same. Lazarus and Seersucker spread mercy where they could, never staying long enough for people to know them. They became a legend, a folk tale.

Then finally near the end of the 20th century a man named Thomas was Seersucker. A young Irishman who'd stowed away on a freighter bound for Charleston, South Carolina. Thomas had been a Seersucker for many years when they came to Harmony. He left Ireland because of a failed relationship with a married woman he met at the golf club where he was a caddy when he was 18. No one knew of their affair. They stole moments in the clubhouse bathroom and on the weekends in the winter they went to her summer home. Her name was Bethany and they spent long hours talking on the phone. He played rugby in a semi-pro league and she would bring her family to watch him play. After a game, Bethany's husband approached him. He said he thought Bethany was having an affair and he wanted him to keep an eye on her. Thomas said he would. That night Bethany invited Thomas to a hotel room and they made love.

Afterwards she told him that she had a secret. She'd been recording their encounters and showing them to her husband. She wanted him to make love to her while her husband watched. Thomas didn't understand and wasn't sure what to do. One night, he tried to tell his father.

"I've gotten myself mixed up in something," he said.

"Then you better find your way out of it," his father said.

So Thomas hitchhiked down to Dublin hoping to stay with a cousin, but the cousin had moved away and so he slept a couple of nights in the streets. He befriended a few of the buskers on Grafton Street and one of them tipped him off to a cargo ship that was taking passengers for cheap to America. It was on the ship that he met Matthew, the Seersucker at the time, and Lazarus. By the time they reached Charleston, Thomas was wearing the suit.

The months he lived in Harmony were some of the best of his life. He slept under the stars and walked the roads each morning free of worry. At the Starlight Diner they would give Lazarus lettuce and

Thomas free coffee and toast. No one ever knew his name or where he was from, but Thomas was a keen observer of the town's comings and goings. He saw in them a strange honest loneliness that reminded him of home. Sometimes he'd walk with Lazarus back to the campsite early in the evening as the shops closed. The butchers and shoe shiners and ministers locking doors and taking out the trash. In Harmony there was no distinction between the loved and the unloved. They were all lonely, cursed by an American emptiness that grew inside each of them. They were convinced their riches were not among them but instead were waiting in heaven. Thomas was a believer too, but not in a distant and mysterious God. He understood and believed in the finality of death. What he'd learned from observing the people of Harmony was they needed something, anything to confirm to them that the world was more than the sum of its parts. When they came to him in the park and asked Lazarus a question they revealed to him their small hopes for the world, and Lazarus gave them a sense that those hopes might one day be fulfilled.

Thomas had shaggy blond hair and looked more Californian than Irish. He loved rugby at school and once read and wept to the poems of Arthur Rimbaud but confessed this fact to no one. He was an only child and wanted to make his father proud. He once dreamed of joining the army like his grandfather but was too scared to take the exam. On his birthdays his mother made him carrot cake, his

favorite, and each Christmas his father cooked a
goose. In his final days, he sometimes dreamed of
going back to Ireland. Of playing video games at his
friend Colin's house. Drinking at the pub. He
wished he could see his family dog again, a dachs-
hund named Rita who always curled up with him by
the fire. He missed the church hymns that he'd
despised singing as a child. He wanted to hike up to
the highest hill in Donegal and watch the sun rising
violet over green pastures. But he also knew that he
had a duty now. He loved Lazarus and believed in
the hope that he gave people. He believed in the
legacy of Seersuckers and he loved to watch people's
faces, especially the children, when they saw Lazarus
for the first time. He thought of himself as the
keeper of a small and important fire that was put
into his care that he was to guard with his life.

The night of the accident Thomas and Lazarus
had been picking apples from a tree near Mulberry
Road. It was late. As they crossed the street Lazarus
saw the car headlights coming over the hill and
Thomas tried to move him, but it was too late. The
car was heading straight for Lazarus, it was out of
control. Thomas stepped in front of the car and
saved his life.

Lazarus now thought of him and his sacrifice. He
could smell Thomas and remembered their mornings behind the Starlight Diner and the smell of
coffee and the nights they spent sleeping under the
stars. He thought of Jill and Quiet and Walt and
Sandy. He thought of Simon and James and all the

rest. And he remembered Eleanor with red hair who wore a yellow bathing suit crying at what they had done and Francois comforting her. He remembered the smell of Little Lazarus on Mulberry Road. As the truck sped over the bridge, Lazarus could see his whole life behind his eyes. The decades became seconds in his mind. The weeks and the years came rushing through him like a wild river as he drifted to sleep.

ELEANOR

I'm at a resort on a private island in the Seychelles with a little rich man I call Sugar. The palms crash softly and the ocean makes a constant noise. Constant waves, constant crash. For me, the clear mountain air is preferable. High mountains, that's for me. Higher the better. So high you could stand on your tiptoes and tickle God's foot. This island might as well be the end of the world. If it wasn't for the money, I might swim away. Sugar is short as most rich men are. I verbally humiliate him and he pays me. This was the arrangement for nearly two months. Then Sugar invited me to this resort. He invited me and I accepted. He cut me a check. A big fat check. A check that was worth about a year's worth of humiliation, all I had to do was spend a week with him down here in the Seychelles. He gave me my own private cabana with an Olympic-sized pool and round-the-clock food and booze. It's well worth the money but I'm starting to hear the sound of the waves in my dreams. It's as if they're stalking me. This morning Sugar comes to my room on his hands and knees and I shame him.

"You're a small hairy man with fat hands," I say.

"I'm so sorry," he says. "I'm so repulsive."

He keeps his eyes to the ground when I humiliate him, but his eyes are heavenly. They're the color of greyhounds. Sugar could be something great if he weren't himself. His whole problem is that he insists on being himself. If he were to snap out of it and become a different man I might develop feelings. I can develop feelings for nearly anyone at any time. There is a deep wellspring of feelings in me. But not for Sugar. He found me on a website. He sent me a nude picture of himself and asked me to tell him everything that was wrong with him and he gave me five thousand dollars. I didn't hold back. He's some kind of billionaire, I think. I never ask too many questions. All evening I sit out on the balcony and watch the stars. When I finally get to sleep I dream of fire. The sky is full of flames.

Sugar calls my room this morning and asks me to come to breakfast.

"I would never eat breakfast with a piece of shit like you," I say.

"I'm sorry," he says. "I'm such a piece of shit."

He hangs up. A few minutes later he calls back. He's out of breath.

"I want to eat breakfast with you," he says. "No more insults for now. I need to ask a favor."

There's a small courtyard between cabanas and the hotel staff set out a vast spread of every imaginable food. I order a strong coffee and sit in the shade. Sugar enters the courtyard in a black t-shirt and pajama pants. I'd never seen a man walk with such weakness. He makes himself a big plate of lobster and steak topped with truffles but can only manage a few bites. Then he pops a bottle of champagne and pours me a glass.

"It's been wonderful getting to know you," he says.

He raises his glass and I raise mine. He looks off towards the direction of the ocean as if mustering the courage to say something. His eyebrows are unruly and his mouth has white spital on both sides.

"I've cheated all my life," he says. "If there was a shortcut, I took it. In every situation I sought an advantage for myself. And I've been successful. Very successful. But those days are over."

I can hear the ocean. Constant and strange. The palms high up in the wind. I take a bite of crab. Sugar takes off his shirt. He exposes his chest to the new morning sun. His chest is thick with gray hair, but his skin is almost chalk white. A small dangling chain holds a single obscenely sized diamond on a ring. He closes his eyes and smiles into the light.

"The sun," he says. "It's good."

He takes the diamond from around his neck and throws it to me and I catch it.

"What's this for," I ask.

I take a sip of champagne.

"I want you to marry me," he says.

I nearly laugh champagne all over his face. The diamond is massive and warm in my hands. He takes a deep breath. From his pocket he gets a small bottle of pills. He takes two and washes them down with champagne.

"Do you like giraffes," he asks.

"I don't dislike them," I say.

"There's a hotel in Kenya that has giraffes that stick their necks through the window and wake you up each morning," he says. "But I much prefer this hotel."

He looks up again at the sky. He seems to put all his hopes and worries there.

"I'm dying," he says.

He starts to talk before I can respond.

"I never believed in free will," he says. "My life was determined. This moment here, with you, it's not a choice you or I made. That's what people don't understand. They think they're in control of their lives, but they're not. Wealth and poverty? Life and death? It's all determined. There's nothing you or I can do about it. It's already happened already. We are riding a wave that began far out at sea."

I smile. Something begins to turn inside me. Sugar is a boy like all the other men in the world are boys. Lustful and afraid.

"You're the only woman that's ever made me happy," Sugar says. "I wanted my son to become a strong man, but he's weak. He needs to know true hardship. I have to leave my money to someone. It might as well be you."

"You're crazy," I say.

"Is that a yes," he asks.

"Yes," I say. "Yes, it's a yes."

He laughs and he looks at me with his greyhound eyes.

"Let's walk to the beach," he says. "I have a surprise for you."

In the distance, a helicopter lands in the field beyond the sand. It drops a large wooden box onto the grass and the hotel staff rush to secure it. They pry it open with crowbars, revealing a large plexiglass enclosure. The helicopter lands and turns its engines off. The island sounds return, the palms and waves.

In the enclosure, sleeping, is a giant tortoise.

"He's all yours," Sugar says.

Two handlers walk the tortoise to us on the beach. The waves brush my feet and the palms crash. One handler is a young man and the other is an older woman. They look exhausted as if they've been up all night.

"This is Lazarus," the young one says. "He's the oldest living animal on earth."

I GO TO MY SUITE AND LIE DOWN AND SUDDENLY I'm back in Harmony twenty-five years ago. I remember Francois. I remember the night on Mulberry Road. I'm back there with such force, I can see everything exactly, as if no time has passed. The palms and the ocean become the moon and the still water of Simon's Pond. I can see my house, green and yellow at the top of the hill. I can see my old red Jeep in the ditch, and I can see Francois. He's wearing a bathing suit and flip flops, a tweed blazer two sizes too big. I try to go back to the moment I first saw him but all I can recall is that morning singing Christmas carols at the nursing home. That morning I'd walked downstairs in my pink mohair sweater and plaid skirt but my father stopped me before I could get out the door.

"You're supposed to wear a red turtleneck," he said.

He wasn't even looking at me. He was glued to the TV. When I didn't reply he turned and looked at me. My mother was at the top of the stairs with Abby. Abby was about to say something but my mother was already telling her not to get involved. That was my mother's philosophy of life. Don't get involved. I could tell my father was getting angry. His eyes went all yellow. His face turned red. There was a thumping in my chest already. A dark thumping that seemed to come not from my heart but from some much deeper place. A throbbing. As if I already knew what was about to happen.

"The choirmaster said you all have to wear the red turtlenecks," my mother said.

"I know," I said. "But I looked stupid in it."

My father got up from his chair.

"Go change now," he said.

"I don't want to wear some ugly turtleneck," I said.

My father was a quiet man on most days but when he got angry he became a different person. There was something secret in his past that no one could know about. It was guilt or shame, something he had done to someone or something that was done to him. I never knew. My father was as big a mystery as God. He worked every day for a man he hated. I used to think that was pathetic. I thought that kind of life was small and embarrassing. It took me years to realize that I should've been mad at the world instead of him.

I opened the front door. It was snowing outside but I didn't dare turn around and grab my coat. I was going to walk to church in my pink mohair sweater, nothing was going to stop me.

"If you take one step outside that door in that sweater," he said.

"What," I said. "What are you going to do?"

Abby came downstairs.

"Just take off the stupid sweater," she said. "He's going to blow up like last time."

She ran upstairs.

"You have to wear the turtleneck," my father said.

"Why," I asked.

"Why," my father said. "It's none of your goddamn business why."

I opened the front door and tried to get out. He came from behind me and slammed it but not before I could wedge my foot in first. I didn't move and pressed the door even harder.

"You're hurting me," I said.

He let go of the door long enough for me to put my leg through and then he slammed it hard. He grabbed my hair and I hit him but he pulled harder and I hit him again in the face and he let go. I ran outside and I kept running. It was freezing but I was running so fast that I wasn't even cold. I didn't dare look back to see if he was following me. I didn't stop until I got to the church parking lot almost half a mile away. It was snowing hard. Really coming down. Everyone was in their red turtlenecks loading up the church van. I was the last one in and sat at the back beside Francois. I knew him from school. His sad eyes and kind face. His eyes were brown and his cheeks were flushed from the cold.

"Can I sit with you," I asked.

He moved over and let me sit down.

"I'm Francois," he said.

"Eleanor," I said.

The bus pulled out of the parking lot and towards the nursing home. I looked out the window and thought about what had happened. I knew I would have to go back there soon enough and face his wrath. I suddenly felt the urge to disappear. I wanted to stand out in the snow and let it pile up until I wasn't there anymore. Until I was no longer myself. Until I was replaced by another girl. A different kind of girl. I turned to Francois.

"Will you take off your coat," I asked.

"Are you cold," he asked.

"Yeah," I said.

I draped it over our laps and guided his hand towards my bare legs. I lifted up my skirt around my waist. He peeked under the coat and saw my bruise. Weeks later I would let him into my room when my parents were away. He was so excited he could barely contain himself. I liked him. Or at least I liked that he liked me. His hands were sweaty and all over me. Grabbing and clawing. Trying to mimic something he'd seen in some late-night movie. I took his hands in mine. They were strong and warm and I held them.

"You can do anything you want," I said. "As long as you do it slowly."

I try to remember back to Harmony in those years. All the lazy days I spent alone. Drifting off into my own quiet universe. The hard thing about being young is knowing what you don't know. Up until that night of the accident I'd believed I could create my own future. Now I don't know. I gave in to the feeling long ago. I let it surround me. After the accident on Mulberry Road that night, I sat there looking at Francois. He was tall with a smooth face, a boy just starting to grow whiskers. When he put on the seersucker suit, he suddenly became a man. We stood there looking at each other, not sure of what to do. Lazarus began to walk through the darkness and we followed him. That's when I had a feeling of the future. I could see it clear as day. I started running away from Lazarus and Francois. It sounds strange but as I ran I saw myself sitting here on this tropical island twenty-five years in the future and Lazarus finding me again. The sound of the palms and ocean. It was all there in the dark woods.

They say two particles can be so entangled they change direction instantaneously from a million miles away. A cosmic dance across time and space. I'm not smart enough to know if that's true. But I like the idea that one moment might be so wrapped up in another, linked forever, that time and space don't matter. No beginning or end but two points in a long orbit, always returning to return. I remember running through those woods that night. I'm back there running now. The moon guiding me through the darkness, I can hear the crash of the waves.

I WAKE TO THE SUN THROUGH THE WINDOWS AND I can barely smell the ocean beyond the palms anymore. I'm lost in two places at once. I'm in Harmony and I am 16 on a roadside and I am 40 and I am on this island. Francois and I are separated by time and space but connected by tragedy, doomed to be linked forever and yet forever apart. Every time I get close again, he's just out of reach. There is nothing worse than remembering joy when misery is at hand. I look out the window and can see the sky is turning. A slight smell of burning wood is in the air. I fear I've manifested fire. I fear the end is near. There's a knock at my door.

"If you don't like the tortoise we can return him," Sugar says.

"No," I say. "I love him."

I open the door.

"He wanted to say hello," Sugar says.

Behind him in the grass Lazarus sits. He seems to contain the whole world. A relaxed and smiling God, bemused by man's folly and despair. I'm transported back again to that night in Harmony then sucked back into the present, lost in the decades, stumbling through the years.

"I need to sleep a little longer," I say.

I close the door and fall asleep. I dream of Abby at the top of the stairs. Her hair in pigtails and her braces and bad skin. We used to spend hours in the basement making up little games. My father built a bar down there and put up a big-screen TV. He said it was for entertaining, but no one ever came over. We made a shop and sold each other our mother's clothes. Her gloves and shoes. We made fake ice cream with glitter and glue, mixing the flavors with spoons and scooping it into Dixie cups. We had dolls but we preferred to play at business. Money was the most important thing to our parents. How they didn't have enough or some other family had too much.

When we were young playing in the basement, Abby and I were the same. Only a few years apart we were like twins. Sharing clothes and crushes and secrets. But as we got into middle school and then high school, Abby changed. She was everything I wasn't. When she made the honor roll, I was failing every class. When she went to the state championship in doubles tennis, I quit the team.

During that time, I became fixated on my body. It was all anyone seemed to talk about. Who was fat and who was skinny. I was always a little bigger than most of my classmates. My mother would make comments about how fast I grew. How I was going to put her in the poorhouse because she had to buy new dresses each year. I came to dread dinnertime. Not just because I couldn't stand my parents but because I hated myself every bite I took. I ate in my room alone each night. Only soup. For months I lived on soup and then just broth. I loved to waste away. I was also tired all the time. I wanted to sit in my room and sleep and forget about the world and disappear.

I could hear my family talking about me downstairs. I would catch whispers. "She has no respect for what I do for her," my father would say. "She's going through a phase," my mother would say. I spent so much time alone that often I would come out of my room to an empty house. They'd gone to the movies but not even bothered to ask if I wanted to go. My parents suffered through meetings with my teachers. They got calls that I was skipping school. Then one day I passed out in Biology class and was taken to the hospital. The doctors said I was dehydrated and suggested that my mother send me to a psychologist. My father was against it.

"She needs structure," he said.

"She needs help," my mother said.

They would fight all night like that. Sometimes I would go into Abby's room. I would walk around and pick her books up off the shelves and read random passages to distract us. We'd try to talk about anything other than our parents. Abby liked math and science and wanted to be a doctor or a marine biologist. She would go on and on about the ocean and the islands and what creatures lived where. I would listen to her even though I was afraid of the water. I hated the thought of what was deep down in the vast nothingness. I was the kind of kid who was scared there was a shark in the pool, Abby was the kind of kid who wished there was one. In those early days before it got really bad, Abby and I were as close as we would ever be. Sometimes, when our parents fought, she would softly scratch my arm and tell me to close my eyes. "Think of the rain," she would say, "it's washing everything away."

Then one morning my father called us down for breakfast and said he'd been talking to the pastor of our church. He called it counseling. The preacher had suggested doing something fun with the family. Where did we want to go on vacation? Abby chose the beach and I chose the mountains, so we compromised with a trip to New York City. We stayed in Midtown and my father took my mother shopping. Abby wanted to go to the Natural History Museum but I just wanted to walk downtown. I kept walking and walking and I was so tired and I didn't know where I was or where I was going.

I kept walking and ended up on 14th Street. I was tired and feeling a little dizzy and nearly fell in Union Square. A man playing chess asked me if I was okay. I said yes but I fell to the ground again. I don't remember what happened next but I ended up in an Italian restaurant. Someone had put a cold cloth on my forehead. A man was there at the table with me. He didn't seem to work at the restaurant but they all knew him. It was as if he was the mayor of that part of the city and everyone deferred to him. He was old and elegantly dressed. A dark wool suit and brown tie. His collar was pressed and he had a navy blue cashmere scarf. Golden round glasses sat perched at the edge of his nose and a black beret was lopsided on his head. Around his neck was what looked like an expensive film camera.

"What's your name," he asked.

"Eleanor," I said.

"Eleanor," he said.

He was quiet as if searching his mind for something.

"Eleanor," he said. "That means light."

"Where am I," I asked.

"You're at Anthony's," he said.

I looked around. There were lonely old people sipping coffee. Outside people were walking against a few early flakes of snow.

"What happened," I asked.

"You fell into my chess game," he said.

"I think I hit my head," I said.

"My opponent was a grand master," he said. "We had to restart the match."

"I'm sorry," I said.

"Not to worry, my dear," he said. "I'm thrilled you're okay."

He looked at me and then back at the window and then back at me.

"The sun is doing something nice to your face," he said.

"How did I get in here," I asked.

He snapped a photo with his camera.

"I brought you here so you could rest," he said.

"They have everything you need here. What do you like to eat?"

"I'm not hungry," I said.

"Nonsense," he said. "You need to regain your strength."

He brought a cigarette out from a pack by tapping it with his finger and then lit it with a silver Zippo lighter. He held up his hand to the waiter and began to speak in Italian. Then he turned back to me.

"I ordered some wine if that's okay," he said. "You're old enough, right?"

"Can I have a cigarette," I asked. I took the cold cloth from my head and put it on the table. A waiter came by and took it away. The man tapped the pack of cigarettes and put one to my lips. I took it and he lit it for me.

"You're not from around here," he said.

"North Carolina," I said.

The food came, pasta and cheeses, and the wine too and we ate without speaking. The restaurant was in the old New York style. Something that seemed to have existed forever. An old gangster joint, maybe, or a place where anarchists hatched plots and drunks died loveless in the corner. All these years later I can see it in my mind. The white table-cloths and waiters in black bowties. I'd fallen like Alice into some kind of dream.

Then the man began to tell me about his wife. How she grew up in Kansas and how she was like Kansas, long and slow. He came to New York to be an artist but his wife wanted him to make money, so he worked on Wall Street and for years she was happy and it made him happy that she was happy, but what he really wanted was to take pictures. And then she died, suddenly crossing the street, and he was devastated but after a few years of grief he thought he should try to finally become the artist he always wanted to be. He was getting a little drunk and was trying to tell me something about how sometimes happiness becomes tragedy and then tragedy becomes reality and then reality becomes happiness again. He wasn't making a lot of sense, but I listened to him and I smoked his cigarettes. He said he took pictures of people on the street. Walked right up to them and snapped their pictures. I'm a hunter of faces, he told me. He only ever took one shot, never more than one, because that's where the heat was, the energy, the passion. He told me he was quite famous in France, where they still appreciated art, but in America he was just another lonely old man. He said America despised artists because they were really free and America hated actual freedom. They only tolerated fake freedom, the freedom to conquer and destroy. Then he said I reminded him of Kansas, which I took to mean I reminded him of his wife.

He touched my hand.

"Maybe we should go to my apartment so I can show you my photos," the man said.

My head no longer hurt but I was a little drunk.

"I need to use the restroom," I said.

I walked to the bathrooms down a long hallway. There was a small tank with a tiny waterfall and a baby tortoise sleeping on a rock island the size of an overturned coffee cup. I looked at him and he started to move. I thought about running away with this man. I wanted to move to New York and be an artist too. I wanted him to take me to France. I wanted to live some other life than the one I'd been given. I thought long and hard about it. My head was spinning but I imagined a future with this man. This widowed photographer. This stranger. Maybe he would take me to his apartment and show me around. And we would smoke cigarettes on the fire escape and play chess and I would tell him about my father and how everything was awful at home. And he would understand and tell me I could do whatever I wanted. I would wear whatever I wanted. I saw a whole new life. Book parties and gallery openings and fine Italian meals.

Then suddenly the next thought came to me. What if this man was a liar? There was no dead wife and he wasn't really an artist at all but a serial killer. A hunter of faces? What was that supposed to mean anyway? I thought of Abby uptown at the Natural History Museum looking at the dinosaur bones all happy, whistling the day away. Then I saw the police coming to my parent's hotel room and saying they found me dead in some crazy man's apartment on 14th Street. Abby would be the sister of the girl who was murdered and it would be my fault because I went with this man. I looked at the little baby tortoise again. He poked his head out of his shell. Nearby there was a swinging door to the kitchen that opened and closed with waiters coming out and I could see there was a backdoor to the place and beyond it an alleyway. I looked back to the dining room. The old man was paying the check in his beret. I realized I didn't even know his name. I stole the little tortoise and ran through the kitchen to the alley and never looked back.

THE SOUND OF HELICOPTERS WAKES ME. THE SALTY smell of the ocean is replaced by the scent of burning trees. I move the blinds and the sky is orange. I watch a helicopter land near the main building and a group of men in suits run out to meet Sugar. I close the blinds and try to sleep but the smell of smoke is everywhere. I open the door to find Lazarus is still there. I'm lost again. My memories and my life have blended together. I try to rest but my mind is full of visions. The phone rings. It's Sugar.

"I want you to know I loved you," he says and hangs up.

I fall asleep and dream of showing Abby the baby tortoise that night in our hotel room in New York. She was the one who said he reminded her of the big tortoise Lazarus, who used to sit in the park with the man in the seersucker suit. We named him Little Lazarus and fed him grapes and watched him crawl across the floor. We stayed up all night making an obstacle course for him with pillows and room service menus and the Gideon's Bible. That was one of my last good memories of me and Abby. Laughing with Little Lazarus in a New York hotel room. Out the window the skyline was lit up and we could see a million tiny people on the street below. For the first time, I talked to Abby about love. She said she had a crush on a boy named Francois. I lied and said I didn't know him.

When we got back to Harmony I told my parents I'd found Little Lazarus in the pond. I thought they were going to get mad but it was the exact opposite. They got him a shoe box and helped us research what to feed him. My father especially. He played with Little Lazarus every night and we talked about him endlessly. A week or two later we found out why.

"Your father and I are breaking up," my mother said as if they were high school sweethearts instead of husband and wife for thirty years.

"Why," Abby asked.

"Your father doesn't want to talk about it," my mother said.

"I'm happy to talk about it," my father said.

And they started fighting and didn't stop until my father left the house. In the weeks that followed my mother didn't leave her room much. I tried to talk to Abby but she only wanted to study. School was her escape. Mine was booze. I never really thought I was drinking that much, it was just something to distract my mind. I couldn't face my crying mother anymore if I was sober. Then one night at a keg party someone slipped something in my drink. I got so drunk I was vomiting in the bushes.

A random girl found me, thank God, took me

home and left me on the porch and rang the doorbell. My mother took me to my room. In the
morning my father was back at home. I could hear
him downstairs arguing with my mother. He spoke
each word with force. As if his words were punish-
ments in themselves.

"Eleanor," he said. "Come down here."

I sat at the table across from him and felt like I
was going to vomit again.

"I wanted to send you away to a wilderness
camp," my father said. "You're lucky it was too
expensive."

"We've decided that you're going to see a
doctor," my mother said.

And so my sessions with Dr. Teddy Holland
began. To be honest, it was a bit of a relief. At least I
could get out of the house. I remember thinking Dr.
Holland looked like 1970's Paul McCartney. He wore
blue jeans and sweaters and drove a little truck that
he parked outside his office which was a little house
on the edge of town. I was grounded otherwise. My
appointments were the only place they would let me
drive my car. So I would leave early and go and
smoke cigarettes by the old stone quarry.

Dr. Holland and I had discussions not just about
me but about the way the world worked. I could see
clear of my problems because they weren't my own.
I began to understand I lived in a place and time
that was not suited for me. The small town American oblivion, it sucked everything into its vortex.
Dr. Holland seemed to understand this, too. He told

me that in his opinion I wasn't mentally ill. Society
made me sick to rationalize its own insanity. Instead
of pills, he used to meditate with me. He would
guide me for hours and I would open my eyes,
deeply relaxed. I thought sometimes he might touch
me. I felt so vulnerable and yet completely safe.

On his walls he had pictures of boats. He told me
he was once in the navy but he never did any killing.
He was a sonar man and only joined because he
loved the water. And when his fellow sailors found
him reading poetry alone they threw his books over-
board and accused him of being a dreamer. He
fought the men that did it and they kicked him out
of the navy and he went back to school. I wasn't sure
why he told me that story except that it was
supposed to show me that he had no respect for
authority.

He told me about cities he'd visited all over the
world. The beautiful places he'd seen. Thailand,
Finland, and Japan. He said things like, "You haven't
really lived until you've seen the northern lights" or
"I've never slept as deep as I did the day I climbed
Kilimanjaro." He was worldly and mature and handsome. At night alone in my bed, I had fantasies
about him. That he would take me away sailing and
he would pour wine into my glass and kiss me, the
wind in our hair. We would get closer in the dreams.
Closer and closer but before he touched me I would
always wake up. It was his idea that I start running.

"You might find it relaxing," he said.

So I bought running shoes and began to run the

trails. Running for me was a total escape. The air filling my lungs and the burning in my legs melted all the anxiety away. I was clean in the world again. For months I ran the trails at McAnderson Park. I stopped drinking and going out with friends.

My sessions with Dr. Holland became like long conversations with a guru. My parents even started to do better. My father moved back and we were like a real family again. One night I was doing dishes and my dad came up behind me.

"I'm really proud of you," he said.

He was almost on the verge of tears.

"I was so worried," he said.

I hugged him and he went upstairs to bed.

That night my fantasy of Dr. Holland deepened. I dreamed up whole lifetimes with him. I began writing them down. Creating houses for us to live in and trips we'd take together to faraway places. I kept my desire to myself. I never told Abby or anyone at school. Seeing him gave me a private peace that no one could destroy. Then one day my mother said I was no longer going to see Dr. Holland. The sessions were too expensive. Before my final meeting I went to the quarry and thought about what to say to him. I knew if I came right out and told him that I was in love with him it would scare him away. So I thought of a plan. At our session I told him how much he changed me, how my life was so much better because he showed me another way of seeing things.

"I hope we can be friends," I said.

"Of course," Dr. Holland said. "I'm cordial with many of my clients."

I drove home thinking about that word cordial. I turned it over and over in my mind a million times. What did he mean by that? Did he mean he wanted to be just friends or something more? I knew Dr. Holland ran the trails on Saturdays. I waited a week so it wouldn't seem obvious then I went out to the trails and stretched in the parking lot until he arrived. I made sure to wear my tightest shorts.

"Eleanor," he said. "Lovely to see you."

My heart got big when he said it. I suggested we run together. We didn't talk much and stayed at a normal pace. Then on the back mile I pulled ahead.

"Come on, old man," I said. "Keep up."

He did his best but I beat him by nearly a full minute. When he got back to the parking lot he was out of breath.

"What took you so long," I asked.

He laughed a little and then touched my arm.

"You looked good out there," he said.

But as soon as the words left his mouth he took his hand away. I thought I was going to fall over and die right there in the parking lot. I knew he loved me too and this was his way of telling me.

"You looked good out there too," I said.

"I better get going," he said.

He got in his car and left. The next week I went back to the trails and waited for him like before. He was stretching and didn't say anything for a second.

"I'm going to run on my own today," he said.

He took off and I followed. I got up close to him and tried to ask him questions. The kind of stuff we used to talk about, but he would only give me one-word answers. Finally he slowed down and stopped near a big oak tree.

"I know what you're trying to do," he said.

"What am I trying to do," I asked.

"I don't want to hurt your feelings," he said.

I didn't believe him and that was the whole trouble. Of course now I can look back and see how stupid it all was. A teenage crush. And I can trace this whole horrible business back to this moment. I could've turned around and run home. Or I could've simply let him run away and none of this would've happened. Who's to say what really matters? I chose that day to put one foot in front of the other.

Dr. Holland ran and I followed. He ran faster and I chased him. The woods were empty and light poured through the trees.

"Stop following me," he said.

"I just want to talk this out," I said.

We ran for nearly two miles at a full sprint until we were both exhausted. When he reached the parking lot he got in his car. I pounded on his car window saying, "Why are you doing this to me? I just want to talk." People were watching.

He drove away. I got in my Jeep and drove home but first I stopped by the old quarry and smoked a cigarette. Then another and another. I thought for the first time of jumping and letting my body sink into the blue water. But instead I drove to Dr.

Holland's house. I parked out front. I wasn't sure what I was going to do. I walked up and rang the doorbell but he didn't answer. I could hear him on the other side of the door.

"You're right," I said. "This is all a misunderstanding."

"You need to go home," he said.

"Please let me in," I said. "I want to apologize."

I tried to open the door but it was locked.

"I don't want to have to call the police," he said.

I started to cry. I sat right down on his front steps and I wept. I wasn't so much weeping for him as I was for myself. Then I stopped. I wiped my tears and drove home. I already knew what was waiting for me. I'd made my choice. When I walked in the door my father was waiting.

"I just got off the phone with Dr. Holland," he said.

But I didn't stop to listen to the rest of it. I walked upstairs and I put on the smallest yellow bathing suit I owned and I ran back outside and got in my Jeep and drove to the lake. I wasn't sure where I was going but I knew there would be a party somewhere. I drove to my cousin Carol's house.

There were a bunch of people there and we went out all day in the boat and it was like old times. Carol was a few years older than me. I always loved her and the way she talked. She talked like all the best people talked. Her hair was cut short and her legs were brown from a summer out on the water.

We sat at the back of the boat and drank beer while the boys did backflips.

"How's life," she asked.

I wanted to tell her what I did. That I'd cried on Dr. Holland's porch. I wanted to tell her that I was in love with him and if he didn't love me back I was going to die. I was afraid. I was afraid of my father. I was afraid of myself. I wanted to run away from everything, but I was too afraid to even do that. I had no real friends. My mom didn't understand and Abby didn't understand. My only joy was the thought of Little Lazarus. The way he walked across my arm. The way he poked his head out when I came into the room. But I didn't tell her any of this. I put my sunglasses on and hid my tears and drank another beer.

"Life's good," I said.

As we came into the dock, I saw someone on the next dock over that looked familiar. It was Francois. I thought he'd been shipped off to boarding school. I waved to him. He jumped in the water and swam to me.

THE SMOKE IS THICK OUT THE WINDOW. THERE'S another knock at the door and I answer and find a man in a pinstripe suit who says his name is Ricky Dives. I ask him where Sugar is and he tells me he's been evacuated. He tells me Sugar is his father and he's sick with dementia. I tell him I don't believe him but Ricky Dives says it doesn't matter what I believe. The island is on fire and soon the whole resort will be up in flames. The last helicopter is leaving and there's only one seat left. I ask about Lazarus. Ricky says there's no time. We have to go now.

"I'm staying here," I say.

"Suit yourself," he says.

I close the door and open a bottle of champagne and lay down. I dream of my Jeep in the ditch near the pond at the bottom of Mulberry Road and I'm back there again. I started to scream but Francois held me. He brought me back to the curb and got a beach towel from the Jeep and put it over my arms. He got another one and put it over the man in the seersucker suit and turned the headlights off. He sat down next to me.

"What do we do now," I asked.

"I don't know," Francois said.

And so we made the decision without discussing it. Quietly and to ourselves. There was no debate. No back and forth. We moved together as one, as if there was a hand guiding us. The man was dead, we were sure of it. I can't remember feeling guilt or remorse, that would all come later. It was pure adrenaline. Nothing went through my mind except the purest of functions. Move here. Do this. Lift that. In retrospect, I've replayed the scene a million times in my mind. I've wondered why we didn't call the cops or call our parents or run to get help or try CPR on the man or drive him to a hospital. I always come to the same conclusion. It was because we both somehow knew, and we both knew the other knew, that it was no use doing any of those things. What was done was done. The events of that night had been set in motion long before we arrived into the world. I pictured Little Lazarus. I wanted to watch him crawl across my arm. I wanted to take him out into the yard. I wanted to be there in the sun with him watching the wind parade the clouds through the sky. I wanted to collapse smaller and smaller into a cell, into a molecule, into the tiniest spark I could become. I wanted to feel nothing and do nothing and be nothing. I kept closing and opening my eyes. Trying to convince myself it wasn't real. Lazarus wandered into the grass near the pond on Mulberry Road to rest. He didn't seem oblivious or ignorant to what had happened. Quite the opposite. He seemed aware of everything. Resigned to the idea that the man was supposed to die this way. The feeling coming from Lazarus is hard to describe. There was a humming, like a low chord played on a church organ. And a faint smell, moss under sunlight or warm water from a summer hose. But there was something much deeper than anything detectable from my senses. A kind of light, glowing weightlessness. The feeling that people hope to feel when they pray to God. Francois stood up and removed the seersucker suit from the man on the ground. We wrapped him in the beach towel and put him in the trunk of the Jeep. Francois put the Jeep in neutral and let it roll slowly into the pond. We sat in the grass and watched it sink.

I can see Francois now in the church van. Tall and lanky in the back seat looking out the window. His blazer had a white pocket square. I loved him but I didn't know how to love him then. I didn't understand yet that love was pain endured together. I love him right now. This minute, I love him. His shaggy hair and tired eyes.

I wake to a thumping at my door. Lazarus is banging his head for me to come outside. The fires are coming closer. He urges me down a path to the pool. I sit with Lazarus and I feel again the weightlessness that I felt that night twenty-five years ago. An elastic feeling as if I was stretching back and forth in time. We watch the last helicopter rise into the orange sky.

I drink more champagne. I try to smoke one last cigarette but my lungs are already full of smoke.

Lazarus paces by the side of the pool as if waiting for someone. I try to tell him no one is coming but he won't listen. I try to move him closer to the water, but he won't move. The fires are almost to us. He keeps pacing. I can see the fire now moving across the resort to the west. Taking each building as it goes. Slowly engulfing them, spreading with the wind. I beg Lazarus to get into the water but he refuses. Soon it will be too hot to even stand here. The heat will kill us before the flames even reach us. I beg Lazarus to get into the pool, the only safe place left.

"Please," I say. "No one is coming to save us."

Then I can see a strange movement from the hills to the east. In the distance, I can see tortoises marching. At first there are only a few but soon I see dozens of them. They make their way towards the pool, slowly but deliberately. The wind makes a path for them through the flames like Moses splitting the Red Sea. By nightfall there are nearly a hundred. Males and females, big and small. Every living tortoise on the island. The ash fills my hair and covers their shells. I pour buckets of water on the flames to keep them away but it's a losing battle. All night we wait as the fires come closer. The sky has gone from orange to thick black. All the lights are gone from the island and the smoke is so thick that it has erased the stars. A hurricane of fire was every-where now, surrounding us. There was nowhere left to go but the pool.

I find a table and throw it in the shallow end and

urge Lazarus toward the water. I ease him in and then go back for the rest. Pushing each one down the makeshift slide. One by one the tortoises fill every corner of the pool. I jump just as the fire overtakes us. We stay in the water as the fires swirl around us leveling my cabana to dust. I know this is the end and I try to remain calm in the face of it. I try to muster some courage, but I can't. The fear and regret consume me. I float on my back looking up at the dark sky as ash rains down like snow and there is nothing but pity. The hours pass slowly and the heat burns my face. I pet Lazarus and he's hot to the touch, I worry he will cook in his shell. I go under every few seconds to cool my face and return to the scorching air.

As I float, I dream of the years after the accident. Much of it was pointless wandering. One town became the next until they were all the same. I washed dishes and waited tables and worked at a dog track and a laundromat and a daycare and cooked meals at a home for the wayward. I did what I could, fucked who I wanted, fought the rest, and made it out alive. I changed my name so many times I forgot who I was. Sometimes I thought about searching for Francois but I didn't know where to start. I thought about him every night when I went to sleep. I hated myself for running. I dreamed of him in the woods and I dreamed of Little Lazarus too. And every night they were consumed by fire in my dreams and now the fires have been made manifest. My dreams and my life have merged into a nightmare.

I wait all night to die. Each time I go under the water I wonder if I should come back for air or simply stay under. But Lazarus is always there. I can't let him be my last regret. I go under one last time and think of the man in the seersucker suit. I see his face in the middle of Mulberry Road, his mouth open to the sky. I think of his mother and his father who never knew how he died or his final resting place. The people he loved who must carry that mystery. And I think of all the tiny ways I could undo what I did. The long sorrow deepens with time. I try to convince myself I had no choice, that it was fate and my will was never free. I'm haunted by the fact that I didn't turn the wheel, that we didn't call someone, that we saved ourselves. I'll never escape that guilt. I come up for air. I want to slip underwater and never come up. But I feel something reaching for me. Something strong. The tortoises surround me, pulling me to the surface once again.

In the morning, I am still alive. The skies are clear. The island is scorched. The resort is gone. Reduced to burning embers. Every building is ash. Only the palms remain, rising heavenward. The waves still beat constantly on the sand. I crawl out of the pool waterlogged and exhausted and sprawl in the sun to dry off. Then help each tortoise one by one climb out into the grass. They wait for an hour or so to get their energy back. We are together. Survivors. Then, as if receiving orders from some invisible general, they march back into the hills where they came from and are gone. Lazarus is the last one. He bows his head to me. I bow in return. He walks alone into the horizon to the soft crashing of waves and the hush of wild palms in the wind.

I'll leave fate and free will to the philosophers. Tonight I'll sleep here in the sand. I'll dream of finding Francois in New York City still alive. I'll dream of returning to 14th Street and walking with him through the past. I'll dream of rainy afternoons down long avenues. We'll be the lover and the beloved. Parading our secrets through the streets. You will become Francois and I will become you. Lazarus will be Little Lazarus. Our dreams will no longer be desires. I will be afraid no longer, for you will be there with me.

LITTLE LAZARUS

NOW ENVISION A FUTURE. AFTER ELEANOR'S disappearance, Little Lazarus lived with her parents in a shoebox on the kitchen table as the neighbors and friends and church folks brought prayers and food. He hid inside his shell and refused to come out. One night Eleanor's mother thought he might be dead and called for Abby to come quickly. Abby picked him up and he seemed to know her by her smell and thought by some miracle Eleanor had returned, but when he saw it was Abby he went back inside. "He wants Eleanor to come back home," Abby said. They looked at each other but didn't speak. They both seemed to know what the other was thinking. Abby put Little Lazarus back in his shoebox and sat with her mother in the growing silence. As that silence grew, Little Lazarus realized somewhere deep down that Eleanor was never coming back.

Now let more time pass. Let Eleanor and Abby's parents get older. Let them sell the house where they raised their children and move into a small apartment. During the move they talked over what to do with Little Lazarus. Eleanor's mom knew she couldn't keep him forever. Caring for him wasn't the hard part. He didn't come out much. Only to eat and to get a drink of water. She called Abby, who was about to graduate from college.

"Maybe we should give Little Lazarus to someone who would really love him," she said.

"I don't know if I'm ready," Abby said. "He's like my last living connection to Eleanor."

So she took him instead. After college Abby and Little Lazarus lived in a tiny apartment in Nashville. These were wild, reckless years. She drank away the grief of her sister's disappearance. Little Lazarus watched from his tank as she brought home men and they always asked the same question. Why do you have this turtle in your bedroom? By this time Little Lazarus was as big as a cereal bowl and his tank required constant cleaning and Abby was often too hungover and didn't have the strength to keep up with Little Lazarus's needs. A smell started to come from his tank. Guys would often mention it in the mornings if they stayed over. Once a guy she really liked, they had gone on a few dates, commented that she should just release him into a pond or something. She never called that guy again. Then another guy told her that it was cruel to leave an animal like that, she didn't call him back either. Finally, Abby met her future husband. He understood why she wanted to keep Little Lazarus. As they became more serious he asked her to move in with him on one condition.

"That we find Little Lazarus a new home," he said.

For days Abby cried at the thought of it. She couldn't let Little Lazarus go even though she knew it was the best thing for him. They fought and fought, but she knew he was right. She couldn't hang on to Little Lazarus simply because he'd belonged to her sister. He deserved a better life. Still the day they drove him out to the animal rescue in rural Tennessee she held him tight. As they rounded the corner to the farm, she whispered to him.

"This is your new home," she said.

She handed him over to the woman from the rescue farm and cried on her future husband's shoulder all the way back to Nashville. It started to rain and the water danced in long elastic shapes on the windshield.

"He's going to have a much better life," he said.

"But is it what Eleanor would've wanted," she asked.

He didn't say anything after that. He just drove with his eyes on the road and pretended to be hyper-focused on the highway. They sat silent for hours then he turned to her.

"I think your sister would've wanted him to be happy," he said.

That seemed to satisfy Abby for the moment, but the guilt over giving Little Lazarus away never left her. As the years went on she would come back to the farm to see Little Lazarus and to bring him his favorite pears. Even if it was hours out of their way, she made a point to visit at least twice a year, around Christmas and on Eleanor's birthday in May.

Little Lazarus was a much more outgoing animal than before and seemed to recognize her and she thought these visits meant as much to him as they did to her. At the farm he was treated like a prince. His name now seemed ironic. He'd grown into a full-sized giant tortoise, nearly five feet tall and almost 500 pounds. He got all his favorite foods and plenty of grass to roam around. After Abby had kids she brought them to see Little Lazarus with her each year. He was a kind of living monument to her sister. Abby would hold her youngest daughter's hand as they learned to feed him fresh pear slices. Her girls fell in love with Little Lazarus and would draw him with green and yellow crayons with thick lines and would ask when they could go see him again. He was mentioned in their prayers each night.

Now we must let even more time pass. Let the cycles of seasons turn with increasing speed. Let the years dissolve into decades. Abby's parents died a few months apart. Abby's children grew up and left for college. The yearly visits became less frequent as she became older. Her husband got sick and after he died her children came to care for Abby. It was harder and harder to make the journey to see Little Lazarus each year. Then one year they couldn't go and that seemed to be the end of it.

But then they began to receive greeting cards with a picture of Little Lazarus from the farm. They arrived on special days. Eleanor's birthday or at Christmas. Always sent with a special greeting in sloppy handwriting as if Little Lazarus himself were wishing her well. But as the years went by, the cards stopped coming. The last one arrived to Abby's daughter long after Abby died. Little Lazarus was turning 90. He was one of the oldest of his kind in North America. Abby's daughter put the card, a picture of Little Lazarus eating watermelon, on the fridge with a magnet in the shape of a balloon and smiled each time she saw him.

The woman who was sending these messages over the years was named Carol. Her father opened the animal sanctuary and she'd tried everything she could to keep it going. Through the years it became harder and harder as the finances didn't make sense. Most of the big animals were gone. They had at one time zebras and ostriches and snakes and one strangely mellow crocodile, Big Fred, who died not long after her father. All of those other animals were gone now. Only Little Lazarus was left. Carol was in her twilight years and needed to sell the land to pay for an operation but she died before she could raise the money. Then bankers arrived and sold off the house and the stables and other buildings. No one even knew Little Lazarus was still there. His corner of the farm was bulldozed to build a parking lot for a new package fulfillment center. So Little Lazarus escaped to the creek and there he lived peacefully near the shore for many years alone and happy. Swimming and relaxing and munching wildflowers. Now use your imagination. Let the years fly by with increasing speed.

Imagine all the possible disasters that will befall

the earth in those decades to come. Earthquakes and fires and floods and the bombs that will fall like rain on the innocent. Use your mind to conjure up the worst of it. The pain, the endless death, and the joy and the sorrow and beauty of the earth exacting its revenge for our greed. See in your mind how astonishingly slow and messy this process will be. The soil drying up over generations and the ice melting and rivers overflowing and the earth opening and swallowing those unlucky enough to still be alive.

Now find Little Lazarus among all this destruction. He is alive among the ruins, enduring. Each day finding the little food and water he needs, his home on his back. And now allow for a terrible fire to begin in the mountains and spread down into the valleys near the creek where Little Lazarus lived out his years. The fire becomes the size of deep ocean waves and it consumes everything. As soon as he smelled the smoke in the distance, Little Lazarus began walking. He walked east toward North Carolina perhaps out of a subconscious magnetism toward Eleanor's home. Danger followed him. A pack of coyotes wandering along a clearing near some old railroad tracks. They attacked him and left bite marks on his shell. Bears and even possums tried to eat him with similar luck. With each attack he would dream of being small again, playing with Eleanor back in Harmony. He thought of being touched again by a human hand. He had outlived all of the humans he had known. They were all gone. Now he only had his instincts and his shell. The fire came closer and closer and each day Little Lazarus had to keep moving farther. He would sometimes wake to find himself surrounded by flames and would have to escape through a narrow path in the trees. Many times he was within inches of death.

Now we must account for time. We must say that many decades have passed and skip ahead to Little Lazarus's final year. For our purposes he is the only living thing that matters. See him there on the scorched landscape. Long past our own deaths. He is still there, surviving against not only the predators and natural disasters but also his own age. He's now the oldest living creature, the last of his kind. Well past a century old. Or possibly two centuries. Or three or four. It doesn't matter. Little Lazarus doesn't understand time in this way. He doesn't feel its passing. To him it's the same continuous life. Seeing Eleanor for the first time felt like yesterday. He moves through the world with no purpose but continuing on each day between the sun and moon. Now the rains come. The rains don't stop. They turn the black wilderness to a muddy ocean. As the water creeps closer and closer Little Lazarus finds a small patch of higher ground. Already this small island is inhabited by a wild dog we'll call Pony. They live peacefully here under a small sandstone outcrop. Pony isn't like the other dogs Little Lazarus encountered through the years. She's a sheepdog and likes to play. Little Lazarus is amused by her and for a few weeks they enjoy an Eden-like existence. Soon the waters rise. All their paths toward safe land are now overflowing with deep brown water. One morning they wake to find the waterline has come within a few feet of their dry outcrop. Pony turns to Little Lazarus and with her eyes seems to ask, what do we do now? But Little Lazarus goes back into his shell. He is old and tired of having to make life-and-death decisions. What comes will come, he thinks. The twilight recedes into an inky darkness. In the morning Little Lazarus doesn't wake and Pony begins to bark at him. The water is only a few inches from them. Then slowly, Little Lazarus rises. He realizes that this dog is the only reason he's getting up each morning.

The water engulfs them that afternoon and takes them away with incredible power into a wide and terrible river moving them toward the ocean. For three days and three nights Pony and Little Lazarus swim. When one of them gets tired the other urges them forward. On the fourth day Little Lazarus notices Pony struggling more than usual. The rain stops and the raw sun bakes them. For a moment Pony is out of sight and Little Lazarus cannot see her anymore. Then she pops up out of the churning water and gives a farewell bark and is gone beneath the waves. Pony will be his last friend.

Little Lazarus holds on for three more terrible days until he finds himself on a beach at night alone. The waves crash over him as the darkness turns into morning. He thinks this will be as good a place as any to rest. Though he loved them, in his final hours he doesn't have any recollections of the many decades he lived with Carol and her father in Tennessee. Nor does he remember Abby or her mother and father. His mind will not allow for any memories to come to him but one. In his final minutes he thinks of the skinny redheaded girl who found him on 14th Street centuries before. He can almost feel her warm hands touching his shell again. His final thought is of Eleanor. Her soft hair and emerald eyes. The waves reach out and touch his feet. Wild and lonely, he lifts his face to the sun.

ABOUT THE AUTHOR

Michael Bible is the author of three novels *The Ancient Hours, Empire of Light,* and *Sophia* and is the screenwriter of the feature film *Dogleg.* He was born in North Carolina and lives in New York City.

www.ingramcontent.com/pod-product-compliance
Lightning Source LLC
Jackson TN
JSHW021556270325
81533JS00002B/127